The Conversation

MIKE GANNAWAY

WESTBOW·
PRESS
A DIVISION OF THOMAS NELSON
& ZONDERVAN

WestBow Press books may be ordered through booksellers or by contacting:

WestBow Press
A Division of Thomas Nelson & Zondervan
1663 Liberty Drive
Bloomington, IN 47403
www.westbowpress.com
1 (866) 928-1240

ISBN: 978-1-4908-8556-8 (sc)
ISBN: 978-1-4908-8557-5 (e)

Library of Congress Control Number: 2015910087

Print information available on the last page.

WestBow Press rev. date: 07/08/2015

DEDICATION

THIS BOOK IS DEDICATED to every person who believed there was something special about my writing, especially my beloved family. I thank you all.

ACKNOWLEDGEMENTS

I ACKNOWLEDGE THE LORD God Almighty as the one who laid this story on my heart. I also acknowledge Regis Lageman of York, PA, and Carol Fox of Manchester, MD as contributors to the editing process of this book.

CHAPTER 1

It is 5:45 pm on Saturday, April 21, 2012, as Diane drives her '98 blue Ford Taurus towards the seaside town of Bethany Beach, Delaware, via DE-26 East. Like many seaside towns, it offers lovely beaches, fancy restaurants, clubs, movie theatres, mini-golf courses, and a boardwalk to attract amusement-starved tourists and their dollars. At the same time, it maintains a very relaxed and quiet atmosphere by having strict limits on business and housing sprawl. It's not an entertainment giant, or nightlife madhouse; only a simple, beautiful place with just enough excitement and energy to allow folks a brief escape from the dreariness of their everyday lives.

She lives only about fifty-five miles away in Dover, but has already been driving nearly eighty minutes. She could have arrived already had she taken DE-1, but decided instead to take a longer, slower route as she is a leisurely driver who wants to relish every minute of the driving experience. The setting sun behind her has created a glorious display of purple, pink, red, and peach on an electric blue canvas that fills her vision as she cruise-controls through the open countryside while listening to a classical piano tape. A few minutes ago she had pulled off to the side of the road to snap a few shots of the sunset with her tiny camera. She has taken numerous photos of evening skies throughout the years, each one distinctive and beautiful. None must ever be lost.

Approaching the ocean, she reaches the end of DE-26 and turns into the northbound lane of Coastal Highway. This is where the town's nightlife is located, and the heaviest traffic is found. Fortunately, it isn't too bad right now since it's still early evening and the tourist season has only just begun; but she still expects to see a fair turnout of people who will be coming to partake in the fun offered by the town.

Driving down the strip, bright signs of a few dance clubs enter her vision and quickly her mind becomes flooded with many memories of an era of her life that existed just over a decade ago. She happily reflects on those times and the joy they gave her.

Back then, from every April through every November, Diane and her two best friends, Cori and Dawn, would get together most weekends and head to whatever club they had chosen to liberate themselves. They were always in perfect synergy and they fed off each other.

They would arrive at one of those hotspots with the tensions and frustrations of life built up inside them, like their hearts and souls were imprisoned in brick and aching to be free. After taking a few minutes to absorb the energy from the music, lights, and other patrons, they would quickly hit the floor to begin the liberation. Over the next several hours the movement of their bodies driven by the energy of the music pulsating through their systems would dissolve the bricks of their inner bondages and purge them through every exhalation and drop of sweat, leaving behind only euphoria.

When it was time to go home, they had poured out everything on the floor and were completely drained, yet the feelings of liberation combined with the intensity of their love for each other gave them a high that no drug could create. They felt so alive, so purified; they couldn't stop smiling or giggling. They had been released.

Yes, those were indeed great times; still, she can't help but laugh at her immaturity in those earlier years. What a meaningless existence that was. Thankfully, as she's matured, she's been able to put away childish behaviors and philosophies.

At 6:08 pm, she slowly veers into the left-turn lane at a traffic light before coming to a stop. After a minute, the turn signal changes, and she crosses the south-bound lane to approach a 24-hour convenience store where she, again, turns left into the parking lot and drives into a space on the side of the building. Through her windshield, she sees the sign saying: *CUSTOMER PARKING ONLY: all other vehicles will be towed at owner's expense.*

Diane quickly switches off her engine, exits the car, locks the door, and closes it behind her. Having been seated for almost two hours she takes a few moments to loosen herself up. Grabbing her left wrist in her right hand and slowly breathing inward she raises her arms straight up overhead while tensing all her muscles. Holding this position, she squeezes her hazel eyes shut and clenches her teeth. A few seconds later she quickly drops her hands to her knees, takes a few deep breaths, and relaxes before standing again to her full 5'7".

She's dressed in a purple T-shirt and black jeans and is barefoot. The 100% cotton shirt fits tautly over her frame; accentuating her broad shoulders, thick upper-arms, V-shaped back and flat stomach. Her bare forearms are well developed and the fabric of her jeans comfortably envelops her muscular legs. A silver ID bracelet hangs on her right wrist. Her dark brown hair, with several gray strands as decorative as tinsel on a Christmas tree, is tightly pulled back in a lengthy ponytail making her strong trapezius more apparent. Soon after shaking the stiffness out of her legs, she heads inside.

This particular store is modernized, with lots of space, soft lighting and wall-to-wall carpeting. It also serves things like lattes, made-to-order sandwiches and fresh desserts. The presence of tables and chairs by the magazine rack clearly suggest this is meant to be a place not just of mere convenience, but also one of social lingering. However, the comfortable atmosphere and tasty food choices don't tempt Diane; all she wants is a single roll of spearmint Certs. She quickly walks to the candy aisle and picks up one.

Walking to the cash register, she immediately notices the cashier's profile: a lovely young woman, black, probably around twenty years old. Her complexion is nearly flawless and her long dark hair is pinned back with a decorative clip and runs down the middle of her shoulders.

Diane has never seen a convenience store clerk look so chic and is quite impressed, but when the clerk turns to face her, Diane finds herself staring into the kindest eyes she has ever seen. Some people would describe them as 'doe eyes,' but while a doe's eyes may be adorable, none could melt a human heart at first sight like the deep brown ones Diane now sees. For a moment she can't move; then she quickly looks down, places the Certs on the counter, and sees the tag on the cashier's black polo shirt: "Lori".

"Will that be all for you?" asks Lori with a voice that matches her eyes. Diane just grins and nods.

"Alright then."

As her order is rung up, Diane thinks of the sea-green eyes of *National Geographic's* Afghan Girl and finds that Lori's are just as equally mesmerizing. Yet instead of the sadness and desperation in the Afghan Girl's, she sees grace and compassion and is astounded that she has found this treasure in such surroundings; much like finding the pearl in the oyster.

"One dollar is your total," Lori says so sweetly.

Diane reaches into her hip pocket for her money clip, pulls out a dollar bill, and hands it to Lori. After depositing the dollar, Lori hands back the Certs.

"Thank you, and have a great evening," Lori says.

Normally Diane would just walk out without saying anything more, but not this time. It's been said that the eyes are the windows to the soul. If that really is true, Diane wasn't about to leave without at least learning a little about who was behind those eyes.

"Thank you for being so kind," she replies.

Lori smiles softly and says, "Not a problem. It's my pleasure," with a tenderness that amazes Diane. She returns the smile with a slight nod of her head. Diane wants to hear Lori's voice again.

"You working much longer tonight?" Diane asks.

"Until eleven," Lori graciously replies, again with that amazing tenderness. "I'll survive, though."

Diane wants to continue the conversation, but quickly senses there's someone else behind her, so she quietly turns and walks toward the exit.

Once she steps outside, Diane instinctively looks back and sees Lori ringing up the order of some skinny guy. She really wants to go back in when Lori is finished, but wisely realizes she might be taken aback, so Diane looks ahead and walks toward the corner of the intersection.

As she's walking, she thinks about Lori and wonders why someone with such dreamy eyes and elegant poise would be working in a convenience store, even a nice one. Maybe she's a full-time student somewhere, and the job helps cover expenses, or maybe she does do something else full-time, but needs the extra work to buy a nice car. It's most likely something like that, Diane thinks.

Even so, is the cashier's job the best she could find? There are a number of part-time jobs out there that are a little more dignifying and less risky. She would be a shoo-in for a department store sales job because anybody who looked into those eyes would gladly buy something just so she'd serve them. Nevertheless, she seemed genuinely happy to be doing what she was doing.

Lori is a real mystery, and Diane wants to learn more, but now is not the time. She came to Bethany Beach with a purpose, and she needs to get on with it. When she returns to her car later, she'll get another chance to see Lori. Diane remembers the camera in her car and realizes she'll need to get Lori's picture, too.

At home, Diane has nearly 400 photos of people she has met in her life: some she has known for years, others were only brief encounters. No matter the length of time, there was something about each one of those people that made them worth remembering, and she wants to remember every face so she can hold on to every memory; which is why she always wants to have her camera on her person because one never knows when an opportunity will present itself. In the case of Lori, her eyes are reason enough to take her picture.

CHAPTER 2

THE LIGHT IS RED when Diane reaches the corner, and she waits. She looks across the four lanes and sees the small seafood restaurant named "Swishy" standing on the corner of the block across from her. When the light turns green, she walks across the highway toward the restaurant and continues along the sidewalk and up a wooden ramp that leads to the beach.

She then steps off the long, wooden planks and onto the sand in front of a wood and wire fence surrounding a grassy sand dune. Walking around the fence, she catches sight of the ocean and runs out onto the beach towards it. The rush of the ocean fills her ears, and the grains of sand wonderfully rub against her bare soles. She slowly inhales the oxygen-rich, ocean air and swirls it around her mouth, tasting its saltiness and releasing it. She does it a few more times and then laughs out loud as the rush of oxygen affects her system like nitrous.

Diane turns from the ocean to face south. To the right of her vision in the distance are the brightly lit boardwalk and its line of sweet shops, arcades, and t-shirt stores that typically adorn others like it along with people heading in and out of them. The area of beach adjacent to it is also brightly lit, and she sees a number of people on the sand. One group is playing volleyball, another has a dog with them, and there are others just sitting on blankets. She is also certain there are a few tipsy people among them. They, like the others on the boardwalk, are all probably having a good time, seeking whatever fleeting pleasures there may be to escape from the banality of the lives they've chosen. Diane pities them, for they do not realize how much amazing wonder is available for their viewing because they choose not to look.

Diane quickly finishes lamenting them and is ready to start her evening, so she turns her back to those lost souls and starts walking northward. Ahead of her, along the top of the shore on her left, are some beach houses. As she progresses, other houses pop up, but she'll eventually reach a point where no person or structure will be near her. Fairly familiar with this section of shore, she knows she'll need about an hour to get where she wants to be. She could've driven herself closer to her destination, but she likes taking long walks on the beach, and there is still a beautiful sunset to enjoy.

Diane walks for about a minute, then unwraps the roll of Certs and puts one in her mouth. Rolling it around causes a build-up of saliva, absorbing the sharp spearmint flavor that eventually stings the inside of her mouth, causing a broad smile to cross her face as she continues walking.

The sky has become a deep, inky blue over the ocean, with the bouquet of bright colors lighting up the horizon over the sand. As she walks, this brilliant spectrum of deep, dark colors will gradually give way to the approaching night. There will be no moon out tonight, so she will be gradually plunged into darkness, which she eagerly anticipates.

CHAPTER 3

ABOUT AN HOUR LATER, the last drop of sunlight evaporates. With the lights of Bethany Beach also well behind her, Diane has no need to continue further.

The landscape is hidden in darkness. She barely sees the white foam of the breaking waves, and her dark clothing keeps the form of her body nearly invisible to her own eyes.

Kneeling down in the sand, she looks up to the clear night sky stretching like an endless canopy over the land and sea. Against the pure, flawless blackness is the very sight she wished to see: the stars. Thousands and thousands of tiny white lights randomly dot the upper reaches of the universe on all sides creating the illusion of being in a giant snow globe having just been shaken up. On most nights, she can count on two hands the number of stars she can see, if she bothers to look, so a sight like this never ceases to amaze her. After putting another Certs in her mouth, Diane slowly rolls down onto her back and places her hands behind her head to take in more of this dazzling display, not minding she's without a blanket.

As she soaks in the enormity of the stars and sky, her mind recalls a poem by William B. Tappan she once read:

> *Fair stars! upon the brow of night*
> *Ye look, from yonder fields of blue,*
> *Where ye, 'mid melody of light,*
> *Bright wheeling worlds! your way pursue.*

Ye never tire,--pure diadems,
The marshalled sentinels on high,
Ye shine, and ever shine, the gems
That fringe the curtain of the sky.

Ye stars! if aught 'tis yours to know,
Beyond your own returnless bourne,
With pity have ye not below
Glanced on these vales where mortals mourn?

O, as I scan your nightly march,
Your anthems steal upon mine ears;
As sprinkled o'er yon glittering arch,
Ye wake the music of the spheres.

Diane has committed a number of poems to memory; especially ones about nature. So often they provide the very words she desires to describe the natural wonders she sees in the world. She's written a few herself, but none have stood up to the masterworks of those before her, so she's left the art to its chosen artists.

Tappan's verses evoke memories of past stargazing experiences: the Great Smoky Mountains, Tangier Island, the Taconic Range, and her first true stargazing experience eight years ago on the prairies of Montana. She had heard for some time that Montana was "Big Sky" country with skies stretching endlessly beyond one's imagination. So one day, on a whim, she just dropped everything, threw together a bag, and took a flight out there to see for herself. After that trip, she would never again view the world and her own life the same as before. Now, here she is today, looking up at that same multitude of stars she saw in Montana, but with far more wisdom and inner peace than she did all those years ago.

The air is comfortably cool; not quite chilly enough that a jacket would be a necessity. The coolness creates a tingling sensation that spreads over her skin like an electric current, causing her flesh to rise and heightening her senses.

The saltiness of the air is becoming more apparent as she deeply inhales it through her nose and then tastes it on her tongue. The salty flavor blends with the spearmint of the Certs already in her mouth, creating a new flavor that is unique to her; one that she enjoys immensely. She slowly exhales through her lips and repeats the process.

Leaving one hand behind her head, she takes her free hand and slides it beneath the surface of the sand and out again. It's so dry and soft to the touch that it comforts her. She pushes her hand back in deeper then lifts it out and lets the grains of sand run over and through her fingers and off the back of her hand, creating a sensation of relaxation throughout her soul. She repeats this process over and over again and soon reaches a calm that's just Zen-like, completely free of tension.

In her calmness, she closes her eyes and shifts her focus from the twinkling showcase to the waves rushing onto the sand. They first hit with a soft booming noise, like many rifle shots fired from a great distance. As they roll away, however, they make a sound that reminds her of when her mother comforted her as a little girl when she cried. '*Shhhhhhhhh*' is what she would say to Diane with such gentle compassion. Diane marvels at how the violent action is followed with a peaceful reaction; the yin following the yang.

At this moment, no one else is here. As far as she's concerned, she's the only person on earth. There is no one else around to bask in all this beauty and voluptuousness; therefore all of this--the night, the stars, the ocean, the sand, the air, the coolness--is all for her...all for her. She is so happy right now.

CHAPTER 4

AFTER SPENDING SEVERAL MINUTES of being washed in a bath of sensation, Diane sits up on the sand, brushes herself off a bit, looks back up at the sky and then out at the ocean, concentrating on it. How strange, she thought. The ocean looked so calm and peaceful in the light of the sun earlier in the evening, but now it's a black abyss: unfeeling, uncaring, cold and filled with horrors. A chill runs through her as she sees it as the perfect visual of Death itself; a sharp contrast to the audio sensation she felt just minutes before.

She reaches down to her pant cuffs, pulls them up, and rolls them above her knees. She stands and walks down to the area of beach the water last soaked. Her feet sink slightly into the wet sand; the water nipping her, alerting her mind to what is coming.

The next wave soon rushes up, surrounding her lower legs, and the icy rush causes her to stand straight at attention, her fingers splayed, her teeth clenched, her eyes squeezed shut and her face wincing. It feels like the cold fingers of Death are digging its claws into her flesh. As the water pulls back, her feet are buried underneath a layer of sand, like Death is trying to take her under. She lifts her feet out of the sand and walks closer to the ocean. Again she gets hit with the same chilled blast of water, followed by the burying of her feet. And again she responds like she did before. Diane repeats this process over and over again, thinking to herself that it is symbolic of how Death regularly comes after her, yet can't overcome her. Someday it will, but only when she's ready to welcome it.

Diane eventually turns away from the ocean and walks back up the beach to dry sand before turning around again and sitting down. Her lower legs are unpleasantly freezing and damp. She rolls down her pant legs and starts rubbing them as hard as she can. It would be nice if she had a towel, thick socks, and a warm room to provide relief, but even without those amenities, she knows her skin will dry eventually and she'll feel fine again. This discomfort she feels only runs skin-deep, and an even greater pleasure will later follow. It's a lesson she learned eleven years ago using cold water.

She was living in an efficiency apartment in North Carolina and had recently read about runners who used ice baths to reduce the soreness in their legs after a long run. Diane was not a long-distance runner, but sitting in icy cold water for a certain length of time sounded like a risk…a thrill…something to conquer, and she believed that true freedom was found in conquest. But for her to go through with this, she couldn't be like the runners who only submerged their legs in the bath while wearing a heavy sweatshirt and drinking hot liquids. It had to be a full-body plunge with no relief available until afterward, just like the Coney Island Polar Bear Club, only in a controlled environment.

So one fall evening she filled her tub deep with cold water and emptied a 20-lb. bag of ice into it. She then went over to the kitchen area, filled her kettle full and set it on a high flame. She spread an extra blanket over her bed and returned to the bathroom with cotton sweats and socks and rested them on the sink.

About three minutes later, the kettle boiled. She hurried over, switched off the flame, and filled up a hot water bottle. After putting it underneath her sheets, she returned to the kitchen area and put a mug with a tea bag in it on her table. She then added a little more water to the kettle and set a low flame under it. Now everything was ready.

Diane undressed in the bathroom and sat on the edge of the tub for what seemed like an eternity, working up the nerve to endure the shock she would receive. The temperature outside was only about fifty degrees, and she had turned off all the heat an hour earlier, so she was already feeling chilly. The thought of feeling an even worse chill was starting to terrify her, and she hated herself for it.

"Don't be a coward! Don't be a coward! It's only a feeling!" she angrily told herself.

When her self-hatred finally gave her the nerve, she removed her wristwatch and laid it on the side of the tub. She then clenched her teeth and carefully slid into the bath, keeping her legs bent as she leaned back so the water level went up past her chest.

During those first few seconds, Diane's eyes squeezed tightly shut, and her mouth sprung open in a silent scream before erratically exerting several short gasps. She shivered uncontrollably and wrapped her arms around herself while trying to breathe steadily. After two minutes, her flesh was in agony, her teeth were chattering, and she could feel her heart pounding, but she continued to endure the anguish. As the minutes slowly slipped by, the feeling of shock faded, and she started to calm down. She was able to resume normal breathing, though she still wanted this to be over.

Throughout the ordeal, she kept checking her watch, waiting for ten minutes to pass, the time limit she had chosen. When it finally did, she leaned forward and pushed the lever to release the water down the drain, then stood up and got out of the tub and back in that now seemingly freezing apartment air. Diane never truly understood what it meant to be desperate for relief until that moment.

When she grabbed her towel, she was whimpering like a little girl as she frantically dried herself as fast as she could. The clothes on the sink were like food to a starved person, and she hurriedly put them on, but her skin was so numb that she felt no immediate relief.

She then walked out of the bathroom to the stove, still shaking and shivering, turned off the flame, and poured the piping hot water into the mug and made her tea. When she started to sip the tea, she winced with pain as it rolled over her tongue and throat. She carefully blew on it and took another sip…and then several more. Soon she felt herself warm up from the inside, and her shivering subsided. Eventually she could feel the soft cotton fabric on her skin and felt such relief that she thought she'd fall off her chair.

She finished the tea and slid into bed, delighting in the pocket of warmth created by the hot water bottle. The weight of the extra blanket embraced her like a lover. The sleep that later followed was the most luxurious she had in months.

Through that experience, Diane learned that positive feelings like relief and luxury, along with compassion, sympathy, and encouragement, cannot be known without first experiencing things like pain, terror, and devastation. Furthermore, it was only through times of testing that lessons can be learned. All of that ties in with what Eastern philosophers figured out centuries ago: positives and negatives are entwined, one cannot exist without the other; the principle of duality. On this particular night, the warmth from her car heater on the drive home is going to feel a lot sweeter than usual; the positive entwined with the negative.

CHAPTER 5

AT AROUND 9:00 PM Diane decides it's time to head back. When she first started out, she had the light of the setting sun. Now, aside from the stars, the only light she can see is from the boardwalk area of where she started almost three miles away. All she sees is a spot of light, but as she walks, it will slowly morph into buildings, structures, and other people. It will be just as visually intriguing as being slowly engulfed in the darkness earlier.

As she walks back, she continues to look up at the stars and begins to ponder the differences of day and night. She thinks of the sky as a window: during the day, it is covered by a curtain, hiding the rest of the universe from the earth, but the curtain is lifted when night falls. On most evenings, the curtain seems lifted only partway, but on special nights like this, when there's no moon, clouds, or city lights, the curtain is completely gone.

Above her is but a miniscule portion of the billions of stars in the Milky Way, which is one of a billion galaxies in the whole universe. Indeed, if the universe were this whole beach, all those stars and planets would be individual grains of sand with the Earth being one of the smallest.

The funny thing is, among those trillions of rocks and balls of gas, this one grain of sand stands alone in its uniqueness. Nothing else has its skies, air, waters, mountains, prairies, and deserts; not to mention its waterfalls, rainbows, and sunsets. But what's even more incredible is that on that one tiny grain of sand are trillions of microscopic particles called living things: trees, flowers, blades of grass, birds, fish, big and small animals, insects, and human beings.

And while she, Diane, is one of trillions of living things on this one of trillions of grains of sand, she can stand alone as magnificent. She has five incredible senses that allow her to absorb information about this world, and a brilliant mind that can store and understand it. She lives inside of a body that is an incredible work of art on the outside and a mind-bogglingly complex machine on the inside. Her DNA has given her a combination of facial and body features that no other human has, ever had, or ever will have.

But what is most remarkable is that she is completely independent of any outside control, thinking for herself and freely making her own choices with her brilliant mind. She has this amazing ability to reason and apply logic to decision-making and she also can feel a myriad of emotions: happiness, sadness, peacefulness, anger, sympathy, fear, desire, etc.; which also factor heavily into the choices she makes.

The irony of it all is pretty hilarious. She is astounded by the size and number of all those heavenly bodies yet she, a speck of dust compared to them, is far more fascinating, complex, and beautiful than all of them put together.

Some would call that arrogance, but she knows it's the truth. It has become so very clear to her in the last few years of her journey yet she takes absolutely no pride in it. How could she? She had nothing to do with becoming a person, but everything to do with the *kind* of person she is now and takes immense pride in *that*. Diane is *free*…and that is by her own choosing.

CHAPTER 6

CHOOSE FREEDOM.

That is the simple two-word phrase that defines the entire being of Diane. As far as she knows, the phrase is her own original creation, although it's highly likely someone else in this world came up with it sooner. It is her life philosophy, her one commandment, the very foundation of the path upon which she has traveled since age fifteen; although she didn't coin the phrase until her early twenties.

Freedom is her greatest desire, and she pursues nothing else: not wealth, not power, not glory, not amusement, not even love. Diane believes the most valuable and precious possession a human can have is total free will: to be in complete control over his or her life, the ability to choose one's own destiny. Choice is what separates humans from the animals. Animals' actions are based on instinct, their bodies reacting to whatever nature has programmed them to do, just like robots. When someone is in bondage, free will is subdued, and control over that life is lost.

The greedy, lustful, egomaniacs, drunks, junkies, perverts, workaholics, hateful, liars…all of them and others alike are in bondage because that is the path they choose. Diane is none of those things because every choice she makes leads to freedom. She chooses freedom. And when freedom is chosen, all the beauty of the world is revealed. People in bondage can never see that beauty; they can only see their bondage. They don't have a choice.

So instead of being burdened by life, Diane is someone who is astounded by it. And why not? She lives in a world filled with beautiful landscapes, incredible experiences, and an infinite amount of knowledge;

where adventure, discovery, and endless stimulation are all available to her at her fingertips every day of her life. And because there is so much available, she's never going to run out of new experiences.

Life is beautiful to Diane. In fact, it's impossible for it to not be beautiful. People in bondage don't realize this reality. There was a time though, when she was in terrible bondage, and that was where this entire journey towards freedom began.

One Monday morning in spring, Diane sat in her eighth grade homeroom preparing for her day of classes when an announcement came over the intercom that a classmate of hers named Jamie (she doesn't remember his last name) was killed over the weekend after being hit by a car. Everyone sat there stunned, and for the entire week, he was all anybody could talk about.

The whole eighth grade was invited to his funeral the next week, and there was quite a turnout, with many students sobbing. Diane was there, too, but she shed not one tear. Jamie was just an acquaintance of hers; nobody she was close to, so she felt no great loss. Instead, what she felt was an overcoming darkness as she was, for the first time in her life, confronted with the reality and certainty of her own death.

For many evenings following the funeral, Diane would retreat to her room and look at herself in her bureau mirror. As she gazed deeply into her own eyes, she saw such light and energy inside them like the flame of a candle. She'd touch her face and feel the warmth of that light flowing beneath her skin. She would then close her eyes and envision herself standing there, alive and well, and then collapsing to the floor in a lifeless heap one second later; as though the Angel of Death came and blew out her candle. Her visible body remained, but the invisible force that was truly Diane was gone forever.

Just like it was for Jamie, a day would come when her light would be forever extinguished. She didn't know when or how, just that it would happen, and she was helpless to stop it. Furthermore, there were many horrific ways by which her demise might come, making her even more fearful and angry.

Death is certainly the great equalizer, she had pondered. If you live a rich and successful life, you die. If you live a poor and lazy life, you die. If you live a selfless, virtuous life, you die. If you live a wicked, hateful life, you die. No matter how one lives or what one does in their life, the end is always the same: you go into the ground taking nothing, not even memories, with you. Nobody has a choice, or a say in the matter.

Death and its inevitability were now constantly on her mind, and the more she thought about it, the more she asked herself, 'Why bother living at all? Why even be born at all?' Indeed, if she just became nothing after she died, just like she was before her conception, what then was the point of living at all? It was a question she could not answer.

Although only fourteen at the time, Diane knew that life was full of struggles, uncertainties, and tragedies. That kind of stuff was all over the media every single day. She didn't see any reason to endure those things if death was always waiting at the end.

It's not that she wanted to be immortal; that would be equally unfair. She believed death should exist, but it should be entirely the choice of the individual as to if or when it happens.

It wasn't long before her helplessness had spiraled into hopelessness and she began to fantasize about killing herself. Death itself might be inevitable, but she could still choose the when and how. She'd die still in control of her life, the master of her own fate.

Furthermore, she decided that she should do it right away. She reasoned that since nothing anyone does in this life will matter after they're gone, it was pointless to delay the inevitable.

She never told anyone what she was thinking, and gave no clue as to what was really going on inside of her. She still looked and acted like the same Diane before Jamie was killed. Had she succeeded in killing herself, nobody would have seen it coming.

She began by writing a suicide note. While she believed her family and friends deserved an explanation, the primary reason she wrote it was to convince herself she was justified to take this course of action. Soon thereafter, suicide opportunities started popping up here and there.

One day while Diane was in the kitchen, she glanced at the block of knives and immediately imagined herself going into the bathroom, filling the tub with water, slashing her wrists, and bleeding out into it. She reasoned it would be a pretty painless way to go; a quiet slipping into a permanent state of unconsciousness.

Another evening, sometime later, she saw a bottle of sleeping pills in a cabinet, and the thought of falling asleep and never waking up filled her mind. It was peaceful and comforting.

Then another evening, sometime later, she was going through her closet looking for clothes to give away and came across a black wool scarf. When she saw it, she thought of hanging herself from her bedpost. No blood, no wounds, and no noise, she figured.

Yet every time she considered any of those possibilities, she would then think of her two little brothers, Daniel and Donovan, who absolutely idolized her. She, in turn, was their fierce protector, ready to kill or die to keep them safe. As devastated as her parents would've been, they were adults and could always have another daughter. Daniel and Donovan, on the other hand, were only children and could never have another big sister. She was it, irreplaceable.

An inner conflict raged inside her between satisfying her own selfish desires and not betraying her brothers. A choice had to be made, and in the end she chose life, which saved them the devastation and her from dying with a guilty conscience. It also forced her to try to find true meaning and value in life, which would free her from hopelessness. Her brothers literally saved her life without even realizing it. She's never told them about her contemplation of suicide, and they don't need to know, but she has since loved them as much as any sister possibly ever could.

Today she now sees that mortality actually makes life a very precious commodity, and every day she's allowed to live must not be wasted. So every morning when she wakes up, she says to herself, 'Carpe diem,' for today is a new day and she has been blessed with another chance to gain something new from this life God has created.

Diane has become a firm believer in the existence of God, a Creator. The knowledge and experience she has gained over these years has made it impossible for her to believe that everything in this universe would just randomly come together and start functioning all on its own. And if God created this universe, it stands to reason He created this world and everything living on it...including people...including her...all by His own choosing.

She believes God created the world for her and her for Himself, delighting in seeing her take delight in all that He's done. That is ultimately how her life can have any meaning and value. It can only happen, however, if she's free from all bondage. Therefore *choose freedom* is ultimately the key to achieving her purpose in life. Trying to reach that point certainly has been a lengthy, yet wondrous process, and she faithfully documents her progress in her diaries.

Diane has been journaling since age twelve, and is presently writing in her 78th diary. Her first one was like that of any other happy preteen girl: thoughts on family, friends, school, her idols, etc. The next three, which covered her early-to-mid teen years, were more serious and moody, especially during her season of contemplating death. But when *choose freedom* began to permeate her soul, her entries started to become deeper and more introspective, with wisdom and understanding increasing as she matured, until finally the words that came pouring out of her mind were so startling that writing became an obsession.

Journaling is now sacred to Diane. She records daily every meaningful and relevant event--people she had met, conversations she had, news stories, books read, movies watched, places visited, sights seen, wisdom gained, bondages broken and to be broken; her whole life written out on paper. Sometimes she's given up entire nights of sleep for the sake of it, filling up numerous pages in one sitting; recording every fact, thought, feeling, and insight until exhausted.

Once in a while, she'll bring a small tape recorder with her when she believes something of great significance will take place. She took one when she went to the prairies of Montana, and how fortunate it was that she did. When night fell and the stars started to come out, she became totally overwhelmed by what she saw, and all these thoughts, insights and revelations came pouring out of her mouth for nearly an hour.

As she listened to herself on the tape when she got back to her hotel later that night, she filled up nearly fifteen pages, realizing she just had a significant breakthrough that opened up a brand new dimension to her philosophy.

She now dreams of one day of using her diaries to write a book about *choose freedom*, providing instruction and hope for the many trying to avoid or escape bondage and discover meaning in life. The diaries are the story of her profound life that will be around long after she's dead, so she gains immortality through journaling.

CHAPTER 7

AFTER YET ANOTHER NEAR hour of walking, the boardwalk area is now coming into view about a half-mile ahead. Diane's legs are feeling a little strained, so she'll need to do a few stretches. She also hasn't forgotten about Lori and still intends to take her picture, in spite of the weirdness of her walking in and asking her to smile for the camera. However, she now has a strong feeling Lori won't mind.

As she gets closer to the artificially lit area of sand, she becomes aware of something else: a man sitting on a blanket looking out into the ocean. He's sitting roughly halfway between the beach-houses and the water line, right in the path of where she's walking. He hadn't been there when she first walked past that area. Perhaps if he had she would've stopped to talk to him, but it's late and she wants to get back, so she doesn't wish to be noticed. Instead she slightly veers to the right to ensure she'll be well behind him when she walks past. As he continues to recline back on his arms looking out at the stars and water, she keeps her eyes on him; he has not once even glanced her way.

When she passes directly behind him, she turns her attention towards the boardwalk, but she stops several seconds later and looks back at him. She can't explain it, but something has overcome her, telling her she needs to talk to him. She tries to take another step towards the boardwalk, but she can't bring herself to do it. She turns herself around to look at him. When she does this, she feels like she can walk again, but only towards him.

Diane wonders what is happening here. She doesn't have time to talk to this guy, nor does she see the point of doing so, yet the desire is undeniable.

This shift in her inner being causes her to ponder her philosophy of keeping oneself out of bondage. Right now she's all wrapped up in how she wants to get back to her car and see Lori again before going home to journal and getting into bed. To simply forge ahead with her plan without even considering approaching him would be an act of stubbornness.

Any act of stubbornness, no matter how insignificant, is bondage because it blinds you to what could be something positive, and she cannot allow herself to succumb to such bondage. Even so, there is no reason to believe he offered anything of value, yet the strong feeling running through her soul is telling her this encounter will not be insignificant. Whether it will be positive or negative, she's unable to decide.

Whatever the result might be, she knows it's now too late to walk away. She has got to talk with him.

She slowly begins to walk down toward him, then stops about thirty feet away and sits in the sand wrapping her arms around her knees. She is not seated directly behind him, but back and to his right, allowing her to remain out of his vision while gaining a limited view of his profile. The light from the boardwalk area is to her back, which is illuminating his right side somewhat.

She's not close enough to discern specific details about his face. What she does realize is that he's wearing a dark dress shirt, khaki pants, and black shoes or boots; way too dressy for just sitting on the beach by oneself. Perhaps he was with someone special earlier this evening…or waiting for someone special to join him. If that were the case, approaching him might lead to an awkward situation. She decides to wait ten minutes to see if anyone comes; if not, she'll approach him.

Diane is not naïve. She's well aware this guy might be an insane rapist just waiting to strike. That doesn't concern her, however; not when she's carrying a switchblade in her right hip pocket, one that she often keeps on her person. If it's not in a pocket, it's in a purse, a boot, or a small holster on a belt.

She purchased the knife at age twenty-two after witnessing a fight break out at an NC State football game where two guys wound up in the hospital. She didn't want to get into any fights, but figured she had to be ready in case one ran into her.

At first, just releasing the blade made her flinch, but after spending a few days getting comfortable with it, she found the knife had given her a brand new boldness that felt so liberating. It was as though she had been released from a bondage she never even realized she was in. She wanted to keep this feeling constant, so she decided to take it everywhere, at least, every place where no one checks for weapons.

She has never once needed to use it and hopes she never does, but she knows she has it in her to plunge it right into the flesh of a rapist, mugger, or any other scumbag that would dare attempt to violate her. Right now, she's resting her hand on her hip pocket, feeling the handle underneath the fabric, and can't help but salivate at the possibility of this guy trying to attack her, and seeing the shocked look on his face when she first cuts him, and then feeling a sense of accomplishment by taking him out of commission. She smiles at her confidence and relishes the feeling of freedom flowing through her right now.

In the four minutes that have passed, Diane has noticed he has not once glanced at his watch or looked around to see if anyone is coming. Perhaps there's no point in waiting out the remaining six; however, moving in ahead of plan could be an act of impatience, and that would represent a loss of control, which would be bondage.

But what other reason would someone have to put on nice clothes and just sit on the beach? It could be he's planning to go to one of the night clubs in the area and wants a little quiet time before he enters that atmosphere, but that doesn't seem likely since there are areas of beach much closer to those places. Perhaps he did come here for a date, and he and his lady friend had already completed it, gone their separate ways, and he is just enjoying his alone time. But it seems a little early in the evening for a date to already be over…unless they had a fight. If he's in a state of sorrow, then it makes perfect sense for him to come out here and console himself. He might be in need of some company.

Then again, he could be feeling very angry. He could be an abuser, and his girlfriend (or even wife) finally took a stand and left him. In that case, she would be better off letting sleeping dogs lie. But she doesn't know what the truth is, and she now wants to find out. And if he is an abuser, then she'll introduce him to her knife.

CHAPTER 8

ANOTHER FOUR MINUTES PASS, and the man still has not looked around for anyone coming, neither does Diane see anyone coming toward him even from a distance. She decides there's no need to wait another two minutes, so she stands up and starts to walk over to him. At first she was going to walk up to his right side, but then realizes she would be standing with her back to the light, meaning he would only see dark shadows on her face. She then quickly and quietly shifts her direction and veers over to his left.

He didn't hear her approach because of the noise of the ocean, so when she suddenly appears at his left side, he quickly turns his head and looks up in surprise, and Diane responds with a soft grin.

"Hello there," she says as she stands with her left hand down at her side and her right thumb hooked into the hip pocket containing the switchblade.

"Hello to you, too," he says rather sheepishly. "Where did you come from?"

Diane quietly laughs as her grin turns into a bright smile. She's feeling a sense of control right now.

"From behind," she replies. "I thought you might like some company. Would you care for some?"

"Yeah, that'd be great."

"Good. One thing though, could we please move over into the light? I can barely see you."

"Oh, certainly."

The man then casually bundles up his blanket and carries it about 20 feet to the right where the border of the light range falls. He quickly spreads it back onto the sand and then sits down on the left side, offering the right to Diane.

While the light isn't that bright, it is illuminating enough to reveal a fair amount of detail of his face to her. He has light brown hair and light eyes, either blue or green. She isn't sure which, but they are gentle-looking. His build looks like that of a surfer or swimmer; just like many of the handsome guys she had encountered back in her days of clubbing. She, Dawn, and Cori were masters of drawing men to them in those clubs.

Cori was a 5'3", raven-haired, olive-skinned Italian with only average looks and a quiet, reserved persona, but she could electrify everybody with her hip-hop dancing ability. Off the dance floor she was an invisible wallflower, but became bold as a lion whenever she set foot upon it, so naturally that's where she spent most of her time. So amazed were the men by her dancing that she only needed to make eye contact with one to get him to come up and dance with her. There were nights that she danced with up to ten different guys without ever saying a word to any of them.

At the other end of the spectrum was Dawn, who didn't need to even step on the dance floor to be noticed. She was a 5'10" blonde, blue-eyed bombshell who could melt a man's heart with just one flash of her beautiful smile. She spent hardly any time dancing with any guy because they all just wanted to listen to her. She had an incredible charisma that drew them in and left them hanging on to her every word. Dawn was the very definition of 'life of the party'.

As for Diane, her well-muscled physique was her magnet. She looked like she had been cut out of a piece of rock and sculpted by Michelangelo. The funny thing was it was created out of a desperate plea for attention.

Her father was a star linebacker for the University of Virginia, and she had inherited his genetics, so she was naturally strong without even lifting a single weight. However, she didn't have the interest in sports that he did, unlike her brothers. She had often felt that he favored them over her, and it only seemed to increase in intensity when the boys started getting involved in sports.

Her jealousy for her father's attention eventually overpowered her sports apathy. So when she was a high school sophomore, she declared she wanted to be a track-and-field star and wanted him to be her personal trainer. He was more than delighted.

They spent numerous hours in the gym together building her strength, with him pouring out praise whenever she reached a new level. The work was hard and tedious, but she had him all to her herself, and his praise meant everything. It gave her the desire to keep pushing herself on the weights to get stronger so she could just jump a little higher and throw a little farther…all for him. She would go on to excel in events like the shot put, the discus throw, and the standing long jump, with her whole family cheering her on.

Diane continued to compete in college, but would call it quits midway through because she never truly loved track-and-field. What she did love, however, was her track-and-field body.

Diane idolized her muscular build: so unique, so healthy, and so perfectly shapely. She loved how she filled out her clothes, especially spandex. She wondered why any woman would starve herself to look like a stick when she could eat her fill and look more like Diane.

Diane had a look that expressed power and commanded respect. She didn't look like some damsel men fought over; she looked like a fighter. And after Diane quit track-and-field, she began to focus on bodybuilding to maximize that look. Not wanting to look like some freak, she never took any muscle enhancers, legal or illegal. Instead she poured through bodybuilding and fitness magazines, selecting the ideal exercise routines and foods to make her ripped and applied them religiously. In just over a year she looked like an Olympian, all 100% natural.

While a few guys didn't find her build feminine, many were fascinated, which is why she often wore sleeveless dresses or blouses at the clubs. She loved it when they ran their hands over her bare shoulders and arms and always got a kick out of flexing for them. While it was all good fun, this fascination would soon lead to guys wanting to get up close and personal.

Her liberation didn't just come from dancing. She had needs that could only be met by the affections of the guys. She craved their caresses, and their kisses made her swoon. These affections, combined with the power of dancing, gave her such an incredible release that many times she was literally brought to her knees.

Diane kissed numerous different men within those clubs: white, black, and every shade in between. She did not discriminate. And while she did value them, it was very shallowly. When she and her friends were done for the evening, she was done with the men, too, never wanting to see them beyond the walls of the clubs. She never gave them her number, and if any of them insisted on giving her theirs, she would throw it away after leaving. Today she regrets how she treated them, and has not pursued a man solely for his affections in a number of years. It will not happen tonight, either.

Besides she can tell that he's younger than her, quite possibly a lot. She hasn't seriously desired anyone younger than thirty since turning that age some time ago, seeing them as too immature. And he looks well younger than the big 3-0. However, that could an act of discrimination, so perhaps she should reconsider that position, though that doesn't mean she should start with this guy.

Even though she won't let the age difference make her uncomfortable, she wonders if it might be an issue for him, if he realizes there is a difference. Diane has never made any effort to hide any signs of aging on her face or in her hair as she has chosen to embrace them as marks of distinction. However, it was unlikely he'd notice any such tiny details here in the limited light; especially when her build is far more noticeable.

Diane still works out regularly, but not for vanity's sake (her chiseled features have smoothed over a bit over the last few years). Instead, her motivation is '*mens sana en corpore sano* (a healthy mind in a healthy body)' as it keeps her free from much disease, depression, and cowardice. She also sees it as maintaining a piece of God's artwork.

In any case, whatever his feelings and observations may be, she would be in control. Nothing would happen in this encounter that she wouldn't permit. Taking a brief glance up toward the heavens, she sits down on the blanket.

THE CONVERSATION

"So what's your name?" Diane asks.

"Chris. What's yours?"

"Diane."

"What's your last name, Diane?"

"I'm not saying, nor do I need to know yours. So, Chris, what's a good-looking guy like you doing out here all by yourself?" she asks truthfully.

Chris happily laughs at the flattery. "Well, I finished spending the evening out with my friends over there," he points at the nearest beach house to them up the hill, "and I decided to spend a little time out here before heading back."

"Are you from around here?"

"No, I'm from Evans City, Pennsylvania."

"Is that far from here?"

"It's in the western part of the state so yeah, it's pretty far."

"And you're seriously going to be driving back there at this hour?"

"Of course not. I could fall asleep at the wheel."

"But you just said you were heading back home."

"No, I said I was heading back…meaning back inside."

If that was an attempt at humor, Diane is unimpressed, although she should've considered that's what he meant. She responds with a sarcastic laugh. "Very funny. Any reason your friends aren't joining you out here?" she asks.

"They decided to go to bed already. I don't blame them, we've had quite an active day and we'll be taking a trip up to Atlantic City in the morning."

"Sounds like fun. Are you heading back in soon?"

"Not anymore," he says with a smile.

She nods in return. "I see. How long have you been out here?"

"About twenty minutes."

"Twenty minutes looking out at the ocean. And what exactly were you pondering during those twenty minutes?"

"Not much really, just enjoying the sound of the waves…the breaking of the surf…the bustle of the people…stuff like that."

"You like the ocean?"

"Mmm hmm."

"I do too, but only when the sun is out. When night falls it becomes this black, lifeless mass that's just like death, and the roar of the ocean is simply a warning that at any time it can come and swallow you up."

Chris' eyes widen, and his jaw slacks a bit, and Diane is well aware of it.

"Oh…I see," he stammers.

"That came out of left field, didn't it?" she says with a slightly teasing tone.

"Yeah…it did," he reluctantly admits.

Diane grins broadly and snickers. She's brimming with confidence now.

"It was something I was pondering earlier this evening. You see, in this area you have the lights, the boardwalk, the people, and the houses; all of which create this atmosphere that renders the ocean as nothing more than a quiet background noise. But you go out that way," she points northward, "and away from all this, where you can't see anything except the stars or hear anything but the ocean; the reality creeps into your mind and then just permeates your heart, leaving you feeling completely chilled inside."

"And what is this 'reality'?" he inquires.

"The 'reality' is the ocean may be the most terrifying thing in existence. Imagine being alone out in that water, far from any land, knowing you could slip under at any second, and your lungs would soon be full of saltwater. And even if you had the unyielding endurance to stay afloat with no chance of sinking, you wouldn't be able to fend off the frightening creatures of the deep that you can't see until it's too late. That scenario is bad enough in the daylight, so imagine the horror of it playing out right now."

"Well, that is certainly profound, but is that why you came here…to create dark scenarios in your mind?"

"Of course not, I came out here because of the stars."

"And what about the stars brought you here?"

Diane gets up on her knees, looks skyward and gestures with her arms.

"First of all, this is the perfect night to view the stars: it's both moonless and cloudless. And second, the beach is one of the few local places where one can view them without the hindrances of trees, buildings, and artificial light; which is why I was over there viewing them," she says as she points northward again.

"I never realized that before. So did you have a fun time?"

"Oh, it was amazing. It doesn't matter how many times I see that display, I'm always blown away. Plus a moonless night only happens once a month, and not all of them are going to be cloudless, so the rarity of those conditions make every experience that much more special. It's an opportunity that can never be wasted.

"There's this documentary I once saw called "The Endless Summer" where these guys spend a year traveling the earth to surf, and I remember this one guy, after spending time at a South African beach surfing many 'perfect waves,'" she uses air quotes, "was lamenting about all the perfect waves that had appeared at that beach but were never surfed, never utilized. That's how I feel about nights like this, they must not be wasted."

"I see," Chris replies. "How long have you been stargazing?"

"For the last eight years."

"Oh, so this fascination didn't happen during childhood."

"Nope, it happened when I was thirty." Diane then sighs in embarrassment, rests her hand across her face and grimaces underneath. She had just revealed her age; not what she wanted to do. She'll just have to roll with it.

"Well, I suppose you just figured out my age," Diane admits and then quietly giggles. "That's okay, though. Age is a trivial thing anyway."

"Why should I believe you?"

"Uh, what do you mean?"

"How do I know you're really thirty-eight? For all I know you could be fifty-two and lying about it."

Is this guy serious? Probably not, Diane thinks to herself, but she'll play along anyway. "Do you seriously think I'm lying?"

"Not really, but you could be. Of course, if you show me your driver's license this issue could be settled right now."

Chris smiles at her. She doesn't return it.

"Oh no, that would mean you'd see not only my last name but my address, too, and that's not going to happen. And even if I did fall for your slickness, I couldn't show you my license because I never carry it on my person. Instead, I keep it in the glove compartment so I never forget it."

"Alright fine, but how come you're good with sharing your age but not your last name?"

"Because of how accessible personal information is nowadays. My first and last name might be all you need to find out my phone number and address. Do you see my point?"

"Fair enough. So what happened eight years ago that made you become such a lover for the stars?"

"I had taken a trip out to Montana because I heard it was called 'Big Sky' country, and I decided I wanted to see just how big it was," says Diane, now sitting Indian style. "I flew out, rented a truck, and drove out to some prairieland where there were no buildings, trees, or mountains in sight; just endless, flowing grassland and the sky itself. I had arrived just over two hours before sunset, and so I began to hike through the grass and soak in my surroundings.

"Anyway, it was a clear day and the sky was the beautiful blue it always is, but this was the first time, at least as an adult, that I was actually in awe of it. I was just blown away by how high and vast it was, and how tiny I was in comparison. I had always known in my mind how big the earth is, but that was the first time I actually felt it in here," pointing to her heart. "I swear, as I was soaking in this great magnificence I was filled with deep humility."

"How far did you hike?"

"Not so far that I lost sight of my truck," she chuckles. "And it wasn't all hiking either; I spent some time lying on my back, too. It's much easier to look up at the sky that way."

Chris has to smile at that one. Diane is now perfectly comfortable with him.

"It was an absolutely evocative experience: the color blue completely filling my vision, the sounds of the wind and the scratching of the grass against my jacket filling my hearing, the feeling of the grassy ground supporting my back, the inhalation of the cool, clean air and being able to taste its purities. All of that sensory stimulation created an absolutely heavenly sensation throughout my being that allowed me to be in complete serenity while I watched the sky slowly change colors." She asks him, "Did you notice the sunset this evening?"

"I did," he answers. "It was quite lovely."

"But were you astounded by it?"

"Not really. I've seen countless sunsets in my life, and they've all been equally lovely. Tonight was no different."

"That's how I used to think about sunsets: lovely but not astounding. But when I put myself in a place where all there was to see was the sky, and the only thing to do was to look at it, I soon developed a brand new perspective," she says with enthusiasm. "I remember the sun slowly descending from the heights of the top of the sky down to the ground, watching it get bigger the further down it went and being able to look directly at it without being blinded. All throughout the process the blue in the sky changed to this shade of purple while these colors of pink and yellow gathered where the sun was falling, at first taking up a large portion of the western sky before becoming this narrow band of light on the horizon. Now I know my description doesn't give the experience justice. You have to actually be in that enormous planetarium environment with a willingness to wait for the color changes, and only then can you truly understand the awesomeness of a sunset.

"Anyway, I've gotten off-track. As the sun continued to set, darkness was gradually enshrouding the entire landscape with me included. When it was completely gone the only things I could see were the stars, multitudes and multitudes of stars completely surrounding me on all sides with nothing blocking them. I could even see the Milky Way."

"Was it a cold night?" asks Chris.

"It was a March evening in Montana, so yeah, it was a cold night."

"Weren't you uncomfortable?"

"No, I was just cold. You see, cold is simply a sensation, a feeling. The only way it can make you uncomfortable is if you choose to be uncomfortable."

"Hold on. Are you saying people are uncomfortable because they want to be?"

"Of course not. Nobody *wants* to be uncomfortable; they just think they have to be because they don't realize they have a choice."

"What do you mean?"

"Have you ever heard of yin-yang?"

"Sure, that's the Chinese philosophy of two opposites balancing each other out to create harmony."

"Well, the actual philosophy is far more convoluted, but that about sums it up: yin-yang is the harmonious balance that keeps the universe in order. And if you go deeper into the philosophy, you'll find the principle of duality: for every positive there's a negative and vice-versa. One can't exist without the other; therefore a positive can be found in every seemingly negative scenario. So instead of thinking about being uncomfortable in the cold, I focused on how alive and refreshed I felt, and that made the stargazing experience even more invigorating."

"Well, while I can see why that would've been an enjoyable experience, I can't see the thrills in it or how it could've been as life-changing as you say."

Diane is cheering on the inside. She has just reeled him in.

"It was life-changing because it made me realize the kind of bondage I had been in all my life. You see, I have a life philosophy called *choose freedom*, which means to live a life free from bondage, and up to that point I thought I had it all figured out, that I was as free as a soaring eagle, but that was not the case. I may have found freedom in many small areas of my life, but it still primarily consisted of just enduring the grind of the work week until I could release all that tension on the weekend and then start the whole process over again. In other words, I was just going in circles.

"Well, on that night, as I was looking up at a night sky that I had never found amazing until then, it registered with me that I was trapped in the bondage of ignorance. There were so many amazing things in this world that I was not experiencing because I was just plain ignorant of them: sites, places, knowledge, wisdom, even simple things like picking wildflowers on a summer day..."

"...or looking at stars on a winter night," Chris finishes.

"Yes, exactly," Diane reacts. "When I chose to look beyond my little world of working and waiting for the weekend, that is when I finally understood what it meant to have true freedom in this life."

"Well, freedom is something everybody wants to have. How does this *choose freedom* philosophy work for you?" Chris asks with intrigue.

"Glad you asked. You first need to understand that freedom is the absence of bondage, and that bondage is when you're in a place where something other than your own free will controls you. You see, you have to apply yin-yang to your daily choices in life and realize that there's always a way to freedom and a way to bondage. You then have to discern which is which.

For instance, I have no tattoos anywhere on my body. My skin is completely clean. Now let's say I choose to have the words 'choose freedom' tattooed somewhere on me. Well, I would be in bondage because my skin would be permanently marked. I couldn't make it clean again even if I wanted to. If I had it removed there would still be a scar. Therefore, by choosing to not get a tattoo, but instead getting 'choose freedom' engraved on this ID bracelet," holding it up, "I have avoided bondage."

"May I see?" Chris asks.

"Sure," Diane replies.

She holds her right wrist close to his face, and he raises the plate between his thumb and forefinger.

"Hopefully you can see it in this light," she says.

"Yep, there it is in beautiful script," Chris says while rubbing his fingertip across the underside. "What's this on the bottom?" He turns the plate over.

"That's the date I began down this pathway of enlightenment; when *choose freedom* was born into me as one might say."

He stares at the date for several seconds.

"Can you see it alright?' she asks.

He gives a slight nod after a few more seconds and releases the plate.

"Alright, now I'm really intrigued. You actually know the exact date this philosophical change took place. So what did happen on that date?" he asks.

"That was the day I met Todd Franklin, a seventeen year-old senior who became my boyfriend shortly thereafter," she answers.

"And he introduced you to *choose freedom*?"

"No, he introduced me to straight-edge. You know what that is, right?"

"Of course. No drugs, no alcohol, and lots of hardcore punk."

"Correct. That is the straight-edge lifestyle in its most basic form, and Todd epitomized it and then some. He also believed in no casual sex. You see, even at that young age, he had the wisdom to recognize that these things people do for brief pleasure can lead to a lifetime of bondage: addictions, diseases, broken hearts, unwanted pregnancies, criminal behavior; all are bondages created by these poisonous activities."

"Just like keeping your skin free from tattoos."

"Exactly."

"I'm curious; did you have an 'x' drawn on the back of your hand all the time?"

"Not all the time, just when we got together with his friends. Of course, I loved having that 'x' on my hand because it was my symbol of belonging...of having an identity."

"So how did straight-edge become *choose freedom*?"

"Todd hung out with a number of older and very hard-line straight-edgers, and he was the only reason I even bothered to hang out with them. These people took such extreme pride in their beliefs that they bad-mouthed others who didn't share them; which, of course, were those that like alcohol, cigarettes, and drugs. That never sat well with me. There were also a few others who had a zeal for things like anarchy, veganism, and even atheism, and I wanted no part of that. So when Todd and I broke up a year later, I stopped hanging around those people, but the values he instilled in me remained.

"The big lesson I learned from him was not just how much freedom was found in keeping one's body pure, but also the strong sense of value one gains by doing so. When I deny myself these poisons that only give a brief period of pleasure, I receive, in return, self-respect because I've decided that I'm far too special to risk being put in those life-destroying scenarios. And it was out of those lessons that the core foundation of *choose freedom* was created."

Diane pauses and sighs. "You know, so much of who I am today is because of him. It's a debt I can never repay."

"What happened to him?"

"I don't know where he is, or what he's doing right now, but I'm not worried. I'm certain his character has kept him out of trouble."

"So what's this core foundation you mentioned?"

"Purity. The whole philosophy of *choose freedom* is primarily built on purity, and it begins with purity of the body. It's the part of your life where bondage is the most obvious, and when you make a conscience effort to keep your body free from poison, you soon become aware of the more subtle areas. In my thirty-eight years, I have not smoked one cigarette, sipped one drop of alcohol, or put a single recreational drug in my system, not even a sleeping pill."

Chris reacts in surprise. "What? Really? You never even tried that stuff before you met Todd?"

Diane nods in confirmation. "That's right. Don't get me wrong, I was curious about that stuff when I was a kid, but I didn't want to risk getting in trouble. I was content to wait until I was of legal age; that was until I met Todd and began to realize the value of refusing to ever take any of it. I remember when I sat down and made a list of all the impurities I had never put into myself and how proud I felt after the list was finished. I realized right then how such a lifestyle of self-denial could create a sense of accomplishment in me. Choosing to never ever start taking those things was a no-brainer."

"Alright, cigarettes and drugs I can understand, but no alcohol either? You never even had a yearning for those "safe" beverages like wine coolers or juice cocktails like screwdrivers; or even a harmless glass of champagne at a party or wedding?" Chris inquires.

She shakes her head. "No. Never. Being free of any and all impurities has given me a uniqueness that I treasure and would never surrender even if my life depended on it."

"Wow...a drug, alcohol, and tobacco virgin. That is very awesome. I honestly wish I could say the same, but I can't." Chris sighs.

"You know," says Diane, "it's funny you mentioned the word 'virgin' because it just so happens..."

"...that you're a virgin, also," he laughs.

Diane just quietly nods and grins.

"To tell you the truth," he continues, "I had a feeling you were when you first said the word 'purity'. You're proud of that, aren't you?"

"Of course I am," she says proudly.

"That certainly makes you a rare gem in this world. What's your motivation?"

"Besides the obvious reasons of being free of a disease, an unwanted pregnancy, and being hurt by jerks who only want one thing; my motivation is how much I value my body. Having sex would mean allowing someone to have complete control over this treasure," Diane says as she points her finger up and down in front of herself. "It would mean putting myself in bondage for someone else's pleasure, and I have yet to meet anyone worthy of such a sacrifice."

"I'm assuming the only person who would be worthy would be your husband."

"That's right."

"I'll tell you what's amazing. The whole purpose of the "free love" movement was to liberate people from the so-called bondages of old-fashioned values like waiting until marriage, and yet that attitude has actually put people into bondage," Chris points out.

"I know," she agrees. "The reason was people only looked at the pleasure they could get. They never once realized what they would have to give up."

"I'm actually a virgin, too," Chris says.

Diane felt her eyes widen a bit upon hearing this. She hoped he didn't notice.

"Really?" she replied. "That makes you a rare gem, as well."

"Why thank you," Chris says upon the receiving the compliment. "However, that doesn't mean I've had a saintly personal life. It is possible to go too far with someone without going all the way...at least, not technically."

"Oh I know," Diane agrees, "and I'm certainly not going to deny that I've had desires that I wanted to be fulfilled. However, those desires can be satisfied through things like kissing, touching, and embracing. All are extremely powerful and pleasurable and you don't need to take off any clothes to experience it."

"Even so, you can still have regrets," says Chris. "I know I have a few."

"As do I," Diane replies. "There have been a few times in my juvenile days where things got a little out of balance and while I may have still walked away pure, I had regrets. But you got to forgive yourself and move on."

"So true," he says.

"Balance is another critical component of *choose freedom*," she continues. "It goes right back to yin-yang: balance equals harmony. Hang on a second." Diane reaches up to her neck and tugs at a thick string around it, pulling up a yin-yang pendant from underneath her shirt. "I wear this to always remind myself about balance." She releases the pendant. "Anyway, I've learned that denying yourself of any physical affection is bondage, just like giving in to temptation only to a lesser degree. We all have needs for physical affection and we need to meet them or else we keep them bottled up inside and that's not good. But when it gets to the point where he or she needs to pull up your shirt to touch you, that's when you get out of balance on the other side. That place of balance is where your needs are met while not submitting to your primal instincts."

"And if you have gone all the way before, your needs become greater, right?"

"Uh-huh. You become weaker to resist temptation which means greater bondage."

"Where else is balance applied?"

"Eating is one area," she says. "You have to eat primarily good clean foods but once in a while enjoy something that is greasy, fatty, or sugary to satisfy those desires. Another area is fitness. You need a balanced amount of exercise and rest to live a healthy life."

"Well, that's just common knowledge. Even I know that."

"Common sense is not so common," she says leaning forward slightly.

"Voltaire," he quickly responds.

"Very good," she says with an impressed tone. "But anyway, the fact is just about everyone knows how to live a healthy lifestyle but few choose to do it, thus they choose bondage, and that's not me."

"So what about marriage?" he asks. "You talk about saving yourself for it, and yet, in a manner of speaking, marriage itself is a form of bondage. It requires the wife submitting herself to the husband till death do them part. Do you want to get married someday?"

"Well, with all the divorces taking place nowadays, you'd think I wouldn't," she answers. "And you're right, marriage is bondage. When you give up being in total control of your own life, and place a level of dependence on someone else, you've put yourself in bondage. However, I have met people who have been married for a long time, and they say it's the best thing that has ever happened to them. And I have to be open to the possibility of getting married for the sake of balance. However, I would have to meet someone absolutely amazing to make me want to give up this life I have now."

"Are your parents still married," Chris asks.

"They are," Diane replies. "Thirty-nine years and counting."

"Mine too…thirty-two years and counting."

"Brothers and sisters?"

"I have an older brother and two younger sisters. How about you?"

"Two younger brothers, twins actually."

"Identical or fraternal?"

"Fraternal, thankfully. The confusion of identical twins would've driven me crazy."

"What are their names?"

"Daniel and Donovan."

"Daniel and Donovan…Danny and Donny?"

She nods. "Yep, that's what we called them when they were little. It was my parents' idea of being cute."

"Are they called Dan and Don now?"

"No, both insist on being addressed by their full names. They don't care for cuteness any longer."

"Do you wish you had sisters?"

"Not at all. If I had any sisters, chances are we would have been competitors. Instead I was the queen: the firstborn and the apple of my father's eye; and my brothers worshipped me," she says with a smile.

"What's the age difference between you and them?"

"Five years. That was perfect for me because I was always bigger than them, and could take them on in fights. I loved tormenting them, and they loved double-teaming me. We hurt each other quite a bit, but it was all in good fun."

"How big are they now?"

"Big enough that they don't need to double-team me anymore," she laughs. "Make no mistake though, the three of us are extremely close and we'd do anything for each other. In fact, the biggest reason I chose to stay local for college was so I wouldn't miss them growing up."

"Where was that?"

"Raleigh, North Carolina. I'm part of the N.C. State Wolfpack. So how were things with your siblings?"

"My brother, Kevin, and I got along, but we were more acquaintances than friends. He's a quiet and reserved person, while I'm more outgoing and we both have different interests. I'm closest with Alyssa, the elder of my two sisters."

"And your other sister?"

"Tessa was a surprise, born more than four years after Alyssa. Everybody spoiled her rotten, including Kevin. He seemed to be most comfortable with her, probably because of the nine-year age difference."

"You know," Diane says, "you are so fortunate to have an older brother, someone who is your protector and confidante. I would've loved to have had an older brother."

"You needed protection?" he asks.

"We all do," Diane answers. "I was the twins' protector and am thankful for it. However, I never had the same blessing. There are some things that happen in life that can only be shared with an older sibling, a protector, and I just had to keep all that stuff to myself."

"Somebody has to be the first-born," he points out. "And besides, not all sibling relationships are good ones."

"I know," she replies. "But I still would've wanted that chance. It's alright, though. I think I've turned out pretty good. Say, are any of your siblings married?"

"No, none of us are. How about your brothers?"

"Daniel's been married for the last seven years and has two sons. Donovan got married last August."

"And you're fine with your little brothers getting married before you?"

Diane nods and confidently says, "I am. We've all chosen our own paths and are happy for one another. At both their weddings, I was a bridesmaid who felt nothing but pride and admiration for the men they had become, and they're both married to good women, so how can I not be happy? As for me, I could go out tomorrow and find someone to marry if I wanted, so it's always an option. I'm not because I freely choose not to be."

"Have you ever been close to being married?"

"You could say that. In my lifetime, I've been in four serious relationships, Todd being my first."

"I'm assuming the other three were fine with your views on intimacy."

"They were. I wouldn't have bothered getting involved if they weren't. My second one was in college and it lasted nearly two years; the third was about six years ago and it lasted seven months; and my last one ended two years ago after three months together."

"Anything bad happen?"

"No, they were all good guys who treated me with respect. It's just that none of them were truly worth giving up my freedom. What about you? How many serious relationships have you had?"

"I've had two: my high-school sweetheart, and one that ended about eight months ago. My sweetheart went all the way down to Louisiana to go to school and quickly decided that was where she wanted to live for always. I didn't wish to relocate, so we parted company. The second one was a rather bitter breakup."

"Oh really," Diane says with keen interest. "What happened?"

"Well, when I met her she was this quiet, soft-spoken, humble person; but then she became very controlling, using guilt and manipulation to have her way. She regularly criticized me, constantly telling me how I was coming up short even though I was doing all I could to please her. And when I quietly confronted her on it, she would become defensive and say things like 'you hurt me' and 'you don't care'." Chris leans back, takes a deep breath and continues.

"Finally, I couldn't take it anymore and I called her up and told her it was over, just like that. At first she didn't believe it, but when it clicked that I was serious, she pleaded with me to reconsider. And when I said I wouldn't, she started screaming at me, asking how could I do this to her and saying I betrayed her. Sadly, that was the last time I spoke to her."

Diane can sense genuine grief in his voice. She's tempted to reach over and give him a comforting touch, but restrains herself.

"Wow, I am so sorry," she says with compassion. "That is so unfortunate. Do you have any guilt?"

"I did for a while. I admit that I'm not without blame. I did allow her to control me and put up with it a lot longer than I should have. But I also know that it was the right thing to do and I have finally forgiven both her and myself," he says with confidence.

"That's good. You know, bitterness is a huge bondage and forgiveness is the only way out of it, and quite often the hardest person to forgive is oneself," Diane says, recounting the time it took to for her to forgive herself for ever considering suicide.

"It sounds to me like she had some serious emotional issues and was looking to you to be her savior," she continues. "Of course, since you're not perfect, you fell short of her expectations, and so she criticized you.

But I agree that you did the right thing; although I wish I could hear her side of the story."

"Fair enough," he says acceptingly. "In any case, that's the biggest reason why I'm not seeing anybody right now."

"I understand," she says sympathetically, "but don't allow it to put you in bondage, or you may miss out on the one with whom you're meant to be with."

"Thanks, I appreciate that," he says gratefully. "Anyhow, you've said *choose freedom* involves keeping yourself poison-free and maintaining a life of balance. What else is there?"

"A lot of humility is involved, also. It's humility that keeps you free from a lot of huge bondages, starting with materialism."

"Oh yeah, that's an obvious one."

"Yes, it is obvious, and many people know it's a form of bondage; however, few are free of it. It's similar to how so many people know that eating good foods and exercising daily will keep you slim, yet so many are overweight because they simply don't apply what they know. You need some kind of breakthrough moment when what you know in your mind becomes what you believe in your heart."

"And did you have a 'breakthrough moment' in regards to materialism?"

"I did. Would you like to hear about it?" she asks.

"Go right ahead," he replies.

Diane shifts onto her stomach. "I was twenty-five and had been working as a paralegal for two years making decent money and was now ready to finally buy my first new car, something I had been wanting ever since I started driving. So one day I was at this dealership, and there in the showroom was a brand-new Chevrolet Camaro convertible, fiery red and gorgeous. I knew it was out of my price-range, but I at least wanted to sit in it, so I asked if I could, and they allowed me. I sat down in those cushy leather seats and looked at all those feature buttons on the dash and envisioned myself owning this car and how awesome I would feel driving it everywhere, and how impressed everyone else would be.

"But then I started to think about all those large monthly payments I'd have to make for the next three to five years; not to mention how much it would cost to insure such a vehicle like that. Then there's the fact that such a car would be a target for thieves, and the worry that would go along with it.

"And then there were all those wonderful emotions I was feeling about possibly owning it. Well, the more I thought about it, the more I realized that after about a year, all those emotions would be gone. The car would become common to me, and all I'd care about is whether it could me from point A to point B. I couldn't have been sitting in that car for more than three minutes. When I got out, I no longer wanted a new car. I wound up driving my '89 Buick another two years; then a '93 Toyota for another five; and now I'm driving a '98 Ford; all of them paid for without a dime of borrowed money."

"And you don't care at all about their luxury or what others think about them," Chris says.

"I don't," Diane replies.

"That's impressive. I'm assuming you get a different car whenever a need for major repairs arises."

"Yep. It's easy to do when you have no emotional attachment to the vehicle and are content to just get rid of it. And it wasn't long after that moment in the Camaro that I realized this principle doesn't just apply to cars, it applies to all material possessions."

"How else have you applied it?" he inquires.

"Furniture is one area," she continues. "In the place I'm staying, I maintain a bare minimum of furniture. If I had to move I could fit every stick of it in the back of a pick-up truck. And most of it is used so I could junk it anyway if I wanted to. The only possessions I value are my clothes, my diaries, my photos, and my laptop. Everything else is not a necessity."

Chris laughs at her statement. "I have to ask, do you ever have company over? It sounds like there's nothing for anyone else to sit on."

She smiles at him in return. "There's enough for one other person, which is why I never invite any more than that over. Just know that while there's not much to look at, I do keep a very clean house."

She continues. "Of course, it's almost always me getting an invitation to come over somewhere. It's like I get to borrow their space whenever I get invited. Borrowing actually helps prevent you from being materialistic."

"Are you kidding me?" he asks in surprise. "It's greed that drives our government to borrow tons of money it knows it can't repay."

"I'm not talking about money. I never borrow money because if I did I'd be under the control of the lender until I paid it back, which is why I'll only accept money as a gift. I'm talking about borrowing things like clothes, books, or a vehicle; stuff that can be returned whenever the lender asks. My point is the less you own the less materialistic you are."

"But wouldn't constant borrowing annoy people?"

"If I kept borrowing something repeatedly, then I'd just buy one for myself because obviously I'd have a genuine need. I'm all for owning the things you need but never going beyond that. And if you can borrow it, then all the better."

"Well, what about housing? Do you buy or rent?" he asks.

"I've always been a renter when it comes to housing, never a buyer," replies Diane. "Now I know some people will tell you that it's far smarter to own a house because it's an asset, and you're not at the mercy of the landlord if he raises the rent. However in that case, one would be at the mercy of the mortgage payments, property taxes, and home repairs. And if things suddenly go south in your life you will then be at the mercy of trying to sell the house, or worse, a foreclosure. When you're renting, the most you lose is your security deposit."

"But renting still puts you in some bondage as you just mentioned," Chris counters. "You can't live bondage-free unless you're living in a tent or a cave."

"And if you did, you would then have to contend with the disadvantages of no electricity or running water," Diane responds. "There are pros and cons with nearly every choice you make; that's not the issue. The issue is how much control over your life each choice leaves you. When you're a renter, you have the freedom to just get up and leave anytime you want with minimal consequence. You could even leave your furniture behind and it would be your landlord's problem to get rid of it."

"That does happen sometimes."

"Leaving furniture behind?"

"Yeah, furniture that's old, worn out, and not worth taking. But it's not right to just leave it with your landlord, even if he does get to keep your deposit."

"I'm not saying it is right. I'm just saying you're free to do it if you want. You never know when something will come up to cause you to leave town ASAP."

"I guess renting a furnished room is the best living arrangement out there," he says.

"Precisely," she agrees. "Someone else has already bought you all your provisions, there's no reason at all to crave more. I spent about nine years living in a furnished efficiency apartment down in Raleigh and I loved it. All I brought in were three suitcases and two boxes and that's all I left with, too. Furthermore, the only bills I had to pay were rent and phone, and the only other responsibility was keeping the place clean. You couldn't wish for a better set-up."

"And when you left, that is when you moved up here?"

"It was."

"Well, what brought you here?"

"Quite a few reasons, actually." Diane sits up again to look at him more directly. "My decision to leave Raleigh was made in the months following my trip to Montana. I had come to realize how juvenile my life had been up to that point, and I needed to break free from it and start anew someplace else.

"I had two wonderful friends, Cori and Dawn, and we used to spend almost every single weekend together going to clubs, parties, anywhere there was a good time to be had; burning off all the drudgery and frustrations of the workweek together."

"Wait a second," he says in a bit of surprise. "You went to all these wild places and never once had a drink?"

She shakes her head.

"Why would you put yourself in such risky situations?"

"Because I know me. I don't crave what I've never had."

"What about your friends?"

"They consumed some alcohol, but only enough to loosen them up. They never once got drunk or high."

"But they knew your beliefs," he says.

"I told them I didn't mind because I knew I would never succumb to temptation," she replies. "Anyway, we had some exciting times together, but as our twenties wound down, I began to tire of the club scene. It was still fun, but it was really starting to seem meaningless to me; and besides, I couldn't keep living that life forever.

"And around that time Dawn had met a great guy named Shane and started spending a lot of time with him, so soon it was just me and Cori going out. Now understand something: Cori is the best dancer I've ever known, so it's impossible to not have a fun night at a club when you're with her, but it wasn't the same without Dawn. She had this charisma that gushed out of her and created a joyful aura that we'd fall under whenever we were together. It was amazing. She could instantly change the atmosphere of a room just by walking into it. Cori and I, I'm sorry to say, just don't have colorful personalities, so something was definitely lost when Dawn stopped coming with us regularly."

If Diane were totally truthful, she'd admit that she was the least important member of the trio. Their atmosphere of energy and excitement was created almost entirely by Cori and Dawn. She was just fortunate enough to be along for the ride.

"And then came Montana?" Chris asks.

She nods. "And then came Montana. When I got back, I knew my days as a clubber were over. I now knew that the key to freedom was not burning off the drudgery; it was not succumbing to it in the first place. I didn't know it at the time, but it was a moment of enlightenment when I realized there was so much to experience, discover, and learn beyond my little world of making a living and partying on the weekend. It was the beginning of my breaking out of that bondage of ignorance. Therefore, it only made sense to move away and start life anew in a fresh location. Besides, both my brothers had already moved away, so there wasn't much reason at all for me to stay anyway."

"You still had your two friends," he points out.

She explains, "Dawn and Shane were engaged at that point, ready to start a new life, and Cori still loved the club scene which I was ready to leave. We loved each other, but our lives were now way different. It was definitely time for a clean break from the old life."

"But why Delaware? Why not move to Montana?"

"I'm an east coast girl, plain and simple. For me, Montana and all of 'Big Sky' country is a beautiful area to visit, but it's not where my heart is. As for Delaware, it's a quiet, inexpensive place to live and just a short trip to Philadelphia and New York City; not to mention a lovely ferry ride en route to Atlantic City. That was enough for me."

"Still keep in touch with your friends?"

"Oh yes. I talk to them both maybe once every month. Dawn is now a happy wife to Shane, and they have three beautiful girls. And in case you're wondering, they do not want any boys. Dawn is a total girly-girl who always wanted daughters, while Shane is their hero who relishes their adoration. To them, the girls have already completed their lives, and there's no need for further additions."

"That's so sweet. I only want to have daughters, too," Chris says.

A slight expression of surprise crosses Diane's face. "You do? How come?"

"Honestly, I don't know," he replies. "It's just a desire that's been in my heart ever since I began thinking about having kids."

"Sons don't appeal to you?"

"No, not really. I mean, if I did have a son, I'd raise him up to be a good man, but I just see myself raising girls more. Call it destiny. What about you?"

"I have no preference; although I do see myself raising boys more than I do girls. Having two little brothers and not being much of a girly-girl has that effect on you, I guess."

"So what about Cori?" Chris asks.

"Ah yes, she's now a member of a hip-hop dance troupe named Sauter de Joie, which is French for 'dance for joy'," says Diane. "She used to be an ordinary bookkeeper who, like me, only cared about dancing on the weekends. But when both Dawn and I stopped, she stopped, too, because she had no desire to go clubbing by herself. However, the desire to dance remained in her, calling out and screaming at her. So after just two short months of sitting on the sidelines, she made the declaration, 'I am a dancer,' and began looking for auditions, ultimately hooking up with Sauter de Joie all the way down in Tampa, which is where she lives today.

"Understand something, Cori is a really shy girl, so both Dawn and I were stunned that she would do something that bold. But she knew her calling and couldn't ignore it."

"I'm curious, how did she get started in dancing?"

"It started at the age of thirteen when she saw Janet Jackson's "Miss You Much" video and was blown away by all the dancing. From that point on, she was determined to dance just like that. She told us that it was like something was unlocked inside her, and seeing that video was the key. She pretty much taught herself how to dance."

"Seriously? No lessons at all?" he asks.

"Well, in all fairness she does have a gymnastics background and had a few personal mentors. But yes, for the most part, she did it all herself," she replies.

"That's amazing. So what's her dancer life been like?"

"She has performed all over the southeast and in Texas, as well as a few stops in the northern states and Canada. The pay's not good, the travel conditions stink, the practicing and performing have left her in pain and exhaustion, and she loves every bit of it."

"Just how bad is the pay?

"There've been times when she and, on occasion, a fellow troupemate have had to dance in parks and on boardwalks for tips so they could buy food for the next day."

Chris laughs upon hearing that.

"Are you serious? Dancing for tips? That's, like, a total cliché."

Diane maintains her composure.

"Yes, I'm serious, and it is a cliché, just like someone playing saxophone in a train station for tips, but they do exist. And she can rake in thirty to forty dollars in one hour flat. That's pretty nice work if you can get it."

"Oh yeah, it definitely is. That's a great hourly wage, and it's tax-free. It's just hard to believe a shy girl would do such a thing," he points out.

She shrugs her shoulders. "Hey, when you got to eat, you quickly forget your pride. Besides, to her it's just like performing on stage with her troupe, only with a little more intimacy with the audience. Either way, she's making a living through dancing."

"Have you seen her perform with her troupe?" he asks.

"I have," she replies, "when they came up for a festival in Philadelphia about three years ago. They were phenomenal, and I'm not just saying that. After the show, I had the pleasure of hanging out with her and the rest of troupe, and I could tell they were a close-knit bunch. I was just so happy for Cori, that she had a family like that."

"How old is she?"

"Thirty-six, the oldest member by quite a few years. She says she's like the big sister of the troupe, which is actually a bit of a twist since she's the youngest of three sisters."

"Oh. That would make you two polar opposites," he says. "She has two older sisters and you have two younger brothers."

"Yes, I know," she says. "And believe it or not, Dawn is the perfect medium. She's the middle child of three with an older brother and a younger sister."

"Actually," Chris says, "she'd be the perfect medium if she had an older sister and a younger brother."

Diane thinks about that for a second and realizes that's true. Amazing she didn't realize it in the first place. "Hmmm…yeah, I guess that's true. Oh well, nobody's perfect."

"I'm guessing Cori isn't married."

"She's not. With all of her practicing and performing, she doesn't have time for any kind of relationship and says she's going to keep on doing it until she physically can't anymore."

"And what happens after that?"

"Who knows? Maybe she'll be settled down with someone rich by then, but if that doesn't happen, she knows she has a couch under my roof to sleep on for as long as she needs."

"Well, you certainly are a true friend. So what about you? Are you happy with what you're doing?" he asks.

"I am," she replies. "I'm a law librarian now, and it's perfect. I'm intellectually challenged, but I don't need to work overtime, or take the job home with me, thus avoiding the bondage of being overworked. What do you do?"

"I'm a mechanic on a dairy farm."

"You're kidding, a mechanic? Let me see your hands."

He holds them out, and she feels his fingers and palms.

"Hmm," she says, "I do detect some roughness, and your fingers seem strong. I guess you could be telling the truth." She releases them.

"Why would you think I'd be lying?"

"I guess I had already had it in my mind that you were either anything from an account executive to a bartender, you know, something that didn't require manual labor. Maybe it's the darkness."

"I hope that's a compliment."

"It is. You're very handsome and well put together."

"Yeah well, there's quite a few mechanics who are that, too; not to mention construction workers, loggers, plumbers, electricians, fishermen, cattle ranchers…"

"Alright, alright," she says waving her hands in front of her, "you've made your point. I'm sorry." She is genuinely sorry.

"Thank you. You're forgiven," he happily accepts.

"Good. So what exactly are your daily responsibilities there? Is there enough work to keep you busy for forty hours a week?"

"Always. A lot of what I do is perform regular maintenance checks on all the vehicles and dairy machinery; and on a farm with about 300 cows, that's a lot to cover. And when a problem does arise, those checks have to be put on hold until the issue is resolved."

"You know," Diane says. "I pride myself on having lots of knowledge, but dairy farm machinery is not something I'm familiar with. How long did it take you to understand it?"

"Two years of school and one year of being an apprentice. Not much to it."

"Apparently not. That is something I should pursue at some point."

"You thinking of a career change?"

"Not a career change, just simply acquiring the knowledge of the machinery."

"I'm not sure I'm following."

"I'm talking about breaking that bondage of ignorance I mentioned earlier; bursting that small bubble I was living in."

"Alright, but what does learning about dairy farm machinery have to do with it?"

"Let me explain. My time in Montana made me realize how much this world offered and that I was missing out on it."

"Yes, you've said that already," Chris says slightly annoyed.

Diane simply brushes that remark off. "So, from that point on, I desired to pursue knowledge; to uncover as many mysteries and make as many discoveries as I could for as long as I'm on this earth. Through the constant process of learning and experiencing, I am able to grow as a person and live in true freedom."

"And you're saying that learning about dairy farm machinery would be a new discovery for you," Chris concludes.

"Yes, it would," Diane affirms. "Learning about all the intricacies of what you work with would cause me to look upon you in wonder of your ability, to understand it all; and it's living a life full of wonder and amazement that overcomes boredom and redundancy in life. That's choosing freedom."

"So you're saying that living in a constant state of wonder and amazement is necessary to be free. That sounds pretty unlikely, if not impossible. How do you do it?"

"I read a lot of books and pursue many experiences like in Montana."

"What books do you read?"

"History, science, philosophy, religion, classic literature, poetry... anything that increases my understanding of the world and grows me in sophistication and wisdom. Ever since I moved here, I've made it a rule to read at least two books a month."

"I'm going to take a guess that you don't have a television," says Chris.

"Well, yes and no," says Diane. "I do have a television, but only to watch tapes and DVDs, no TV shows. I watch Oscar winners, foreign films, art-house flicks, documentaries -- anything with an artistic or educational element to it. The stuff on TV is just a waste of time."

"I totally agree," he says. "Television can become a drug if you're not careful."

"That is so true," she agrees. "Television is simply a means of escaping from reality. Nothing positive ever gets accomplished from escaping; it just causes life to pass you by. Now I'm not saying a little escapism is bad. Once in a while, I like to kick back for an afternoon with a suspense thriller or western novel, but it can never be what you live for in life.

"For so many people, their lives consist of nothing but grinding it out at work while dreaming about their escape. That's who I used to be; clubbing was my escape and it was the best part of my life. Sure, I had fun, and it was a great release, but it didn't make me into a better person and it certainly didn't make me discover any real purpose in life."

"And what other Montana-like experiences have you had?"

"So far, I've hiked through the Appalachians, danced in the streets of a little Mexican village, seen the Northern Lights in Canada, and the sun set over the Pacific. I've also walked the West Highland Way of Scotland, and tasted genuine New York pizza in Brooklyn. Not bad so far, wouldn't you say?" Diane says beaming.

"That is impressive," Chris says nodding in agreement, "especially the trip to Scotland."

"That was my first trip outside of North America, with more to follow," she says, speaking with excitement.

"What was it like?"

"It was a ninety-six mile long hike, and it sure wasn't flat, but my brother, Donovan, and I walked the entire length in seven days. Our legs were killing us at the end of the journey, and all of our clothes were filthy, but we were both so happy. We saw some of the most glorious landscapes you will ever see in your life. I wish I had my pictures here because I really can't do justice to the mountains, prairies, lakes, and wildlife we saw.

"But it wasn't just the sights; it was also the people we met on the trail and in the little villages along the way. We had such fun swapping stories with the other travelers, the ones who spoke English anyway, and native Scots. I took plenty of pictures of the people, too, and there's a story to share for each one."

"I noticed you only mentioned Donovan," he points out. "Was Daniel not with you?"

"No," she replies, "he was home with his wife and newborn son. I was actually planning on taking this trip alone when Donovan started to call me about wanting to hook up. It eventually led to him joining me on the adventure."

"You didn't ask Daniel?"

"No, I knew with the birth of his firstborn child that home was where he needed to be. Plus, I wanted this to be a special time for Donovan and me only.

"I told you the three of us were close growing up, but Daniel and Donovan were far closer to each other than either of them were to me, and it continued into adulthood; they both got jobs in the same city and became roommates...and yes, that was their plan from the beginning.

Then Daniel fell in love, got married and had a family; meaning Donovan was no longer the most important person in his brother's life, and that was hard on him. So he gave me a call."

"Ah, crying out to his protector for help," Chris says.

Diane can't help but grin at the truthfulness of that statement.

"I suppose there's some truth to that," she says, "but it was mostly because he was forced to examine his other relationships and then he realized he also had this amazing sister whom he rarely saw. And as we conversed, it soon dawned on me just how little I knew my brothers. Oh, my love for them certainly hadn't changed, but I had definitely grown distant from them.

"The five-year age difference was a huge factor because, growing up at home, I always saw them as kids and, as you said, assumed the role of being their protector. That didn't change even when they reached their late teens. Then they were off to Georgia Southern to make new lives for themselves while I was already busy with my own new life, so I never got the chance to create a new relationship with them."

"I see," he says. "You hadn't gotten to know them as adults. So how did things go in Scotland?"

"It was fantastic," she happily states. "For over a week, it was just me and him with no other distractions, so we had no choice but to talk to one another. From the flight over to the flight back and everywhere else in between, we were together.

"As much fun as we had hiking through the highlands and meeting new people, the absolute best parts of the experience were the times when it was just us two talking alone, either on the trail or in one of those little villages along the way. For most of those times we talked about the past, reliving all those childhood memories and revealing a lot of personal stuff that we had never shared. Then, towards the end, we really revealed who we are today. As you said, we got to know each other as adults. And what we discovered was that we genuinely liked each other. We would've wanted to be friends even if we weren't related. Isn't that wild…how you can love someone before you like them?" she says.

"It is," he responds. "So what happened after the trip?"

"We both went back to our lives, but started communicating with each other far more frequently, and it's not out of any kind of family obligation; we genuinely like talking to each other."

"And what about your relationship with Daniel? Did you do anything to deepen it?"

"I called him up shortly after returning home and told him about my time with Donovan, and then apologized to him for allowing our relationship to become so distant. He told me it would mean a lot for us to get reconnected. While I don't talk with him as much as I do with Donovan, I do visit him and his family once in a while, and it's been great."

"Now you mentioned Donovan got married recently."

"That's right."

"Has that caused any change in your relationship?" he asks.

"I may have been a little jealous at first, but I soon got over it," she replies. "It wasn't like it was between him and Daniel where they saw each other every day, whereas we lived in different states. Yeah, he still has time for me just as before.

"There are few things that can compare with having good strong relationships with your family members. You can never be lonely when you have that."

"Well that's awesome, it really is," Chris says. "But were you lonely before Donovan called?"

"Well, I certainly didn't feel lonely," Diane replies, "but when I compare what life was like before Scotland to life after, I really can't say. A lot of bondages are like that, they're so familiar to you that you don't realize you have them. Excuse me."

Diane pulls out the roll of Certs and puts one in her mouth. She rolls it around in her a mouth for a few seconds and then asks, "Oh, you want one?"

"Yes, please," Chris says, taking one and putting it in his mouth. "I needed that…all this talking." There's a pause in the talking for a few seconds and then he asks, "Actually, are you thirsty? We can go in and get something to drink."

Immediately a sense of caution flooded Diane's being. Her common sense is telling her that could be dangerous, but her switchblade gives her confidence. She maintains her outer countenance.

"Uh, that's a little forward, don't you think?" she cautiously inquires. "Inviting somebody you only met half-an-hour ago into your house. In fact, it's not even your house. Kind of impolite of you, I'd say."

"I'm only asking you to come in for something to drink. It won't take but a few minutes," he says reassuringly. "And I'm welcome to anything in the refrigerator, so my friends won't mind me sharing some."

"Yeah, but aren't they going to mind you bringing a total stranger into their house? If I were one of them, I'd at least be a little concerned."

"Well, I have a good feeling about you," he jokingly replies. "Look, you don't have to come in if you don't want to. I just figured you might be thirsty."

The truth is, she's quite thirsty, plus he does look and sound sincere. So she decides to go ahead, figuring the switchblade will be enough protection.

"Alright, fine," she accepts. "If your friends do get upset, it'll all be your fault anyway."

The two of them stand and walk up the sand to the beach house deck. Chris slides open the door, and the two enter the living room. The room temperature is noticeably higher than the outside, which is a nice break from the coolness. He flips a switch, and immediately the room is softly illuminated by the ceiling light.

It looks about as cozy as one would expect from a beach house. The walls are painted light beige, and the hardwood floors are stained dark. On the right is a stone fireplace with an oil painting of a snowy wooded area at sunset. Against the left wall is a long wood table with an empty crystal vase, a collection of bookended novels, and a framed family photo on its surface.

In the center of the room is a large, white area rug with a two-seat sofa on its left side and two large comfortable armchairs on its upper and lower right corners with a marble-topped coffee table in the middle.

"Is there anything in particular you want?" Chris asks.

"Water is fine, but if you have any fruit juice, I'll take that," Diane replies.

"Sure, back in a minute."

"Actually, I'd like to come and see the kitchen."

"Oh, alright."

They go to the other end of the room and exit through a doorway on the right-hand side. Chris switches on the light. They walk across the hardwood floor which continues from the living room.

The kitchen sink, refrigerator, stove, microwave, cabinets and drawers are all contained in a little area fenced off by a long, island granite countertop. The rest of the room is empty except for the round, wood kitchen table and chairs placed against the right-hand wall with curtained windows.

Chris goes to the stainless-steel refrigerator and pulls out a bottle of apple juice, placing it on the island. He then gets two glasses from the cabinet over the sink, fills one with water and the other with the juice. All the while, Diane doesn't take her eyes off him even for second.

After putting away the bottle, he walks over, hands her the glass of juice, and leads her back into the living room. She did not witness him slip anything foreign into her glass. There is a possibility he already drugged the bottle of juice, but she isn't so paranoid to seriously consider it. He gestures over to one of the armchairs.

"Please sit down," he says to her.

Diane steps on the rug and finds relief in its softness. She happily sits down and relishes the luxurious comfort the chair provides. Chris sits across from her on the couch.

She's thankful to finally see him in normal light. Just as she had thought, he looks like a surfer, although she doubts a dairy farm mechanic from Pennsylvania has ever even touched a surfboard. Perhaps hockey player would be a more appropriate description. Even so, he definitely looks like somebody she would have approached in a dance club. The big difference here is they are actually conversing.

She had danced with, kissed, and touched so many great looking guys in those days, yet had not one meaningful conversation with any of them. None like this, anyway. As she gets settled into the chair, Diane feels this is a night of redemption, a chance to make up for all those lost opportunities. She takes a sip of juice.

"This is a nice place your friends have," she says looking around. "What are their names?"

"Kenny and Alexa," he replies. "This place actually belongs to Kenny's parents. They were going to be away for the week and invited the two of them to stay here. You know, to be house-sitters. At the last minute, they decided to let me join them for the weekend."

"They went on a vacation?"

"Vermont. It's quite lovely up there in spring."

"I'm sure it is, but you know what's truly odd?"

"What is?"

"That the three of you would come here for a vacation because those two were leaving here to go on a vacation."

A confused look crosses Chris' face. "I'm not following."

Diane explains. "So many people would consider this house and this location a vacation spot and that to live here would be like being on a lifelong vacation. Yet your friend's parents who do live here don't see it that way. Instead, they felt a desire to get away from here for a while. It's like someone who lives in the Bahamas wanting to get away to Florida for a while. Do you understand what I'm saying?"

"I believe I do," he says drinking some more water. "You're saying that when a place becomes your home, no matter how beautiful and relaxing it is, your perspective of it changes. It's no longer a place to get away from it all."

"Oh, it goes beyond that," she continues. "It's a case of what you once saw as beautiful has now become common and ordinary because you see it every day. It eventually becomes about as interesting as, well, the scarcely furnished place I'm renting!"

Diane laughs for a few seconds before taking another sip.

"Uh, please be quiet," Chris admonishes. "I don't want them to be disturbed."

"Oh, sorry about that," she humbly apologizes.

She kicks herself for that moment of childishness. Now if his friends walk in here upset, it'll be her fault.

He says to her with a smile, "Now if my friends walk in here upset, it'll be your fault."

He just read her mind! How did he know? Well, she won't let him keep the upper hand.

"You have appropriately administered correction; quite mature for someone your age."

"Ah-ha," he says lowering his head. "I really don't know what to say to that."

"Trust me, it's a compliment," she responds with renewed confidence.

"Alright fine," he says unconvinced.

"Chris, I'm two years shy of forty. Have you even reached thirty yet?"

Chris looks a bit humbled now. "No, I haven't," he says.

"Then I can say something like that. It's no put-down, just something I can say."

"Well then, thank you for the compliment."

"You're welcome," she says taking another sip.

Diane has recovered quite nicely and is now savoring it. She then turns and looks behind her, before turning back around.

"Excuse me a second," she says.

She gets up and walks over to the fireplace, examining the painting above it.

"You like it?" he asks.

"I do. It brings to mind a poem by Robert Frost. He's a particular favorite of mine. It's called, *Stopping by Woods on a Snowy Evening*. It wouldn't at all surprise me if that poem was the inspiration for this." She turns and looks at him. "Have you ever read it?"

"Can't say that I have. What's it about?"

"It's about a man on a horse-drawn sleigh who stops to observe some woods on a snowy evening."

"Hence the title," he sighs. "Why didn't I realize that?"

She giggles. "It's alright. Anyway, the curious thing about it is the man says the evening is 'the darkest of the year', yet he stops to observe his surroundings. I wonder how much he could've seen."

"I don't know," he says, "but I recall a number of evenings where the snow actually brightened up a landscape. Of course, they were all clear evenings with the moon out and that wouldn't be the case if it were snowing. One thing's for certain, that painting was unlikely inspired by that poem because it's not snowing and the sun's still out."

"That's true," she admits. "Good observation."

"What other Frost poems do you know?"

"To name just a few: *Mending Wall*, *Fire and Ice*, *A Question*, and *The Road Not Taken*."

"Hey, I know that last one. It talks about *the road less traveled*."

"Yes it does. In fact, it's one of my inspirations for *choose freedom*."

"Because it's about choice?"

"Right…and looking back on the choices you've made that have gotten you to where you are now. When breaking free of bondage, one has to look back and recognize the choices he or she made that put them on that path in the first place."

"Mmmm hmmm, learning from one's mistakes. Does *the road less traveled* lead to freedom?" he asks.

"Of course it does," she replies. "I've learned that the path of least resistance, the one that most people take, almost always leads to bondage. Freedom has to be earned and fought for. It takes hard work and self-denial and that is *the road less traveled*. You think it was easy for me to maintain purity for all this time? It took a lot of discipline, but it was all worth it."

"Speaking of purity," Chris says with a slightly humorous tone, "did you know that apple juice has a lot of sugar in it and sugar is bad for you?"

Diane slams the palm of her left hand across her chest and grits her teeth.

"Ooooooo…you got me there!" she says smiling at him. "I guess I need more discipline."

He just raises his glass to her and drinks. She walks back over and sits down.

"You know you had that coming," he tells her.

"I suppose I did," she says finishing her juice. She wipes the bottom of the empty glass dry on her pant leg and sets it on the table.

"Thank you again, for the juice," she says as she curls her legs up underneath her.

"Would you like another?" he asks.

"Oh no, I'm fine," she replies.

"Alright. So anyway, Robert Frost is a favorite of yours. Why does he appeal to you?"

"His poems are inspired by nature and I love nature. He had a particular fondness for New England landscapes. In fact," looking behind her, "that painting right there resembles such a landscape. You said Kenny's parents are vacationing in Vermont right now?"

"Yes," he says.

"Hmm, that's interesting," she comments.

"Why is that?"

"I don't know. I mean, they're vacationing in a part of New England, they have what is likely a New England landscape hanging on their wall, Robert Frost writes poems inspired by New England landscapes, I love Frost's poems…it's as though I was predestined to be in this house."

Stop right there. Don't cross that line, she tells herself.

"Oh, what am I saying?" she says with a somewhat embarrassed tone. "I'm sorry, I am way overanalyzing this."

Chris looks back at her very thoughtfully.

"No problem," he says. "So you were talking about why you love his poetry?"

"I love it because he focuses so much on nature and rural life, absorbing as much as he can out of creation and putting it down in beautiful verse. It's just like how I am with stargazing, or any of my Montana experiences, except he didn't have to travel as much as I did. He also can write way better poetry than me, and while I envy that, I know my adventures are far more ambitious than anything he could've imagined."

Chris seems indifferent to that statement.

"What other Montana adventures do you hope to experience?" he asks.

"Well, there's backpacking through Europe, visiting Angel Falls in Venezuela, standing on top of Table Mountain in South Africa, just to name a few," she replies.

"Sounds expensive."

"It is; however I'm free from materialism, remember? And I make good money at my job, so I save, save, save. I also know that I'm never going to go every place I want in my lifetime, but that's how it should be. I will never run out of things, or places to experience."

"Regarding materialism, you don't have to buy anything to be materialistic. You can become materialistic about cash and never spend it or give it away. I once read about a couple who had bags full of cash in their place, and yet starved to death because they didn't want to spend it," Chris offers.

"That's an extreme case of stinginess and is, indeed, a form of bondage," Diane concludes, "which is why I gladly give away part of my income every month to avoid it."

"Oh really," he remarks. "Who do you give to?"

"The Salvation Army, March of Dimes, things like that," she answers. "I even carry extra cash on hand in case I meet anyone in need of it. And, let me tell you, it's always a joy to give them something."

"You just got it all covered, don't you?" he says to her in a somewhat serious tone.

"Well, I don't know about that, but I think I'm pretty close," she replies in a slightly puzzled tone.

"Do you mind if I make one comment, however?"

"Alright."

"Are you familiar with the phrase, 'there's nothing new under the sun?'"

"Yes, I've heard it."

"Well, this philosophy that you've taken such pride in creating. I just don't see anything groundbreaking or revolutionary about it," Chris states. "I mean no smoking, drinking or drugs; no premarital sex, no overspending, shun TV; read lots of books, do lots of traveling, don't waste time because life is short. All of those tidbits of wisdom have been around for many years and have been practiced by many. It's great that you, too, put them into practice, but you're certainly not the one who came up with them."

"I never said I came up with them," she explains. "What I'm saying is that I've discerned what choices lead to freedom and have willfully chosen to make them. And perhaps many have made a few of those choices in their lifetimes, but how many would you say have taken it to the extreme I have?"

"I'd say not many."

"And I'd say you're right," she says with a smile. "*Choose freedom* is no joke, my friend. It's the belief that freedom is the most important possession a human being can have and is worth giving up everything else to keep. And when I say 'everything,' I'm talking about wealth, success, love, fleshly pleasures, reputation, entertainment, security, and all that other good stuff people sacrifice their freedom to obtain. *That* is the philosophy by which I live and don't you dare just dismiss it."

"Alright," he says holding up his hands to signal 'stop'. "You have made your point. I apologize for making that crack, but let me ask you this: All this striving you do to learn new things, gain more wisdom, meet new people, traveling the world, and breaking bondages--what does it all mean in the end?"

"Excuse me? Haven't you been listening?"

"I have...and I'm talking about the end of your life. No matter how much of this freedom you obtain, at some point you will die just like everybody else. So what then will all of it matter after you're gone?"

"Now you're talking like a lazy person with no ambition or sense of purpose," Diane says with a hint of defiance. "I'm well aware of the fact that I'm mortal, and you know what I've learned about mortality? It makes life special. Life is a precious commodity that will someday run out, so it must not be wasted. Sounds like you believe that death actually makes life meaningless, and therefore there's no point in pursuing anything. And if that's what you believe, you may as well just kill yourself right now."

"Well, that's brilliant insight," Chris responds sarcastically, "but it doesn't answer the question. I'm asking you: What is the point of your pursuing all this "freedom," as you call it, when none of it is going to matter when you're dead?

"For instance, you read all these books to acquire knowledge, wisdom and understanding to escape the bondage of ignorance. Well, other than making yourself feel enlightened, what's the point? What's the practical purpose of gaining it, other than becoming a more sophisticated conversationalist? The same thing applies to all these 'Montana experiences' you desire. Yes, they may create some great memories for you and perhaps make you feel more satisfied with your life, but beyond that, what else is there? How does any of it create a legacy or make the world a better place? I guess what I'm getting at is: once you're dead, what will any of it mean?"

Diane has to think about this. A few seconds later she has an answer.

"I think I understand," she says. "You're saying that all my laboring for freedom benefits nobody but me, and because I'm going to die, free or enslaved, it's all meaningless in the end."

"Precisely," he concurs. "Look at the lives of people like Thomas Edison or Mother Theresa. Their passions resulted in numerous people being blessed. That's a true legacy, a life worth living. What you pursue sounds like nothing more than vanity."

Diane can't believe what she's hearing. He is actually saying her philosophy leads to a meaningless life. She knows she must remain calm and quietly refute his error.

"Well, first of all, we can't all be brilliant inventors or super-humanitarians, right? Some people are gifted in things like writing books, composing music, or teaching calculus."

"Yes, you're right, and all those things benefit others, which is a legacy."

"Well, my legacy is simply setting an example for living. People look at me and see what a life free from bondage is like. I share with them the wisdom I've gathered and they can go apply it to their own lives. Why, in this whole conversation I've shared a lot of wisdom with you, and surely you'll retain some of it. Furthermore I've recorded all the knowledge and insights I've gained from *choose freedom* in my diaries and my goal is to one day write a book so the whole world can be influenced. Will I have a legacy that will make me a household name? Probably not, but that's not what matters. What matters is *choose freedom* can potentially impact every person I come in contact with, and that includes you."

Chris nods his head and says, "I certainly can't deny that. Alright, you've made a good point, but now let's go deeper. Do you believe in life after death, or is this all there is? Because if we all just become nothing after we die, then you'd have to say life itself is meaningless, and that nothing we do in this life matters."

Suddenly Diane perks up. It's been weeks since she has had a deep, philosophical discussion with anybody, and is she ever hungry.

"Now *that's* a profound statement," she exclaims, "and I totally believe it. If everybody just becomes nothing when we die, regardless of who we are or how we live, then yes, nothing we do on this earth matters. Whether I lived in freedom or in bondage in this brief life won't matter anymore once I'm gone."

"Correct," says Chris. "And what we do unto others, whether positive or negative, won't matter to them after they're gone either."

"Which then brings us to a question what many philosophers and deep thinkers have been pondering for centuries: What's the meaning of life?"

"Absolutely," Chris agrees. "Why are we here? What's the point of it all? But before one can answer that question, he must determine whether life has any meaning at all, and that comes down to one thing: Is there a God? The only way life has any kind of meaning, any kind of value, is if there is a God who chose to make it. Because if what the atheists say is true, that we are nothing but the result of a great cosmic accident and billions of years of random chemical mutations, then there is no purpose at all for our existence."

"So you believe in God?" she asks.

"Absolutely, I do" he answers.

"I do, too," Diane happily admits. "I can't pinpoint the exact moment all my doubt was erased, but I know it happened in my mid-twenties. Before that, I guess you could say I was an agnostic. I wasn't ready to believe in such a thing that was beyond my comprehension, yet I didn't want to be closed-minded enough to dismiss the possibility completely."

"Yeah, I remember you mentioning you didn't want to hang around those straight-edgers who were atheists."

"That wasn't the only reason, but yeah, you're right. Anyway, as I was maturing in *choose freedom*, I was developing this deep sense of self-respect; that I just knew I was of great value. But then I had to ask myself: Why am I valuable? What is it that gives me value? Am I valuable because my family loves me? No, because that would mean, if they didn't love me, then my life would be worthless."

"Precisely," Chris agrees. "There has to be a concrete basis for why all human beings deserve to be treated with dignity and respect. If it's all based on opinion, then no one can make a judgment call.

"Let me tell you about a conversation I had a few weeks ago with a guy who didn't believe in absolute truth. I said to him, 'Alright, let's say the dictator of a third-world country decides to do something about all the starving people in his land, but his solution is to send his army into all the villages and gun down every starving person. Was he wrong in doing that?'

"And he said, 'Yeah, of course he was wrong.'

"And then I asked, 'Well, why was he wrong?'

"'Uh, because he murdered all those innocent people?'

"'But he didn't believe it was wrong. He figured it's better to die quickly from a bullet than slowly starve to death. And another thing, being the dictator also meant he was the law. Therefore, there was nothing illegal about what he did.'

"'But he wasn't justified to kill all those people. They wanted to be fed, not be shot.'

"And then I said, 'That sounds like an absolute truth.' He didn't have a reply to that.

"Anyway, the point is that without some kind of law handed down from a higher power in regards to murder, no one could judge that dictator's actions as evil because that would be, quote, forcing one's morality on another, unquote. The same thing applies to valuing people just because they're people. All people are creations of God, so all people are valuable."

"Very insightful," she says. "We're both fortunate to have realized that already."

"Why thank you," he says. "So anyway, you were talking about what eventually led you to come off the fence."

Diane nods at him. "Ah, yes. Well, while I was pondering what it is that makes me valuable, I also pondered the sheer magnificence of our bodies and their mind-boggling complexities, such as the ability to see. Through the eyes, our brains are able us to tell us all that's around us with crystal-clear perfection, and, without our eyes, we'd see nothing.

"The more I thought about this one elementary fact, the more I realized sight itself is a miracle, and so must be the eye. I recall spending an entire evening at the library researching the intricate and complex make-up of the human eye, and I just knew that nothing this incredible could have been the result of an accident. I can't even fathom an eye midway through its evolutionary process."

"That's a great point," says Chris. "Did the beasts of that time have blurry vision for thousands of years before the eye was fully evolved?"

"That's right," Diane confirms. "And you could say the same thing about the other four senses; each one is just as astounding as the other. Think about it: our ability to detect and differentiate thousands of different sounds, smells, flavors, and textures. There is nothing our minds have created that comes close to that kind of sophistication. Therefore, there must be a greater mind at work."

"And you know what else?" Chris continues. "There are no useless senses. All five of them are critical to understanding our surroundings because there are, as you said, thousands of things to see, hear, taste, smell and touch. It's impossible to fathom all five of those just coming into existence by accident."

"And on top of that," Diane adds, "there's the existence of things like water, oxygen, plant and animal life. All these things we need to survive."

"And how about the ozone layer?" adds Chris. "All this talk about the need to protect it, but does anyone ever ponder how such a thing so essential for survival got there in the first place?"

"Another great point. It just goes on and on, the list of evidence that proves the existence of God," Diane says to him with a smile. "You and I could write a book."

"Well, there's a thought," Chris says returning the smile. "So anyway, it's great that you believe that God exists, but what do you suppose is the next step? Surely, He wants us to do something for Him, or else why bother creating us?"

"I can tell you this much, He wants us to our lives free from bondage," she proclaims.

"Well, that goes without saying, but there has to be more to it," he responds.

"I believe that," she says. "I would say He wants us to experience Him."

"Experience Him? What does that mean…to communicate with Him?"

"It means to sense Him: see, hear, feel, smell, and taste Him."

"What?"

"Does that sound bizarre to you?"

"Kind of, yeah."

"Well, it shouldn't. God is not flesh and blood, so He relates to us differently than we humans to each other."

"I already know that," he argues, "so please get to the point."

"My point is that these five senses which we have are our links to God," she proclaims. "Everything that brings true joy to our senses is from God, and what is from God is also God himself. When I see the rainbow after the storm, I see God. When I smell honeysuckle on a warm summer night, I smell God. When I hear a brook running over stones, I hear God. When I run my hand across a mink fur, I feel God. And when I eat a well-seasoned Porterhouse steak, I taste God. Those are just five of the literally thousands of ways we get to experience God, all of them wonderful. And it's through these experiences that we develop a love for Him."

"Those last two statements tell me you're not a vegan," Chris muses.

"That's correct," Diane says. "I did consider the morality of killing animals for our needs, but then I thought of the Indian tribes of the Great West who needed to hunt the buffalo for their very survival. Since no one condemns them, I can't be condemned either."

"I agree," he says. "If it were really wrong to eat animal meat, then surely God would've poisoned it. Anyhow, what you've described sounds a lot like pantheism. Is that what you are?"

"I'm not anything," she says leaning forward, "and neither is God."

"Well, God is certainly God and nothing else," he admits, "but every human has some set of religious beliefs. Even not having any beliefs is a belief."

"*Choose freedom* is my religion," Diane states. "As for God, He's far bigger than any one faith, or single set of beliefs. In fact, I believe God can be discovered and experienced in many faiths. For instance, you mentioned pantheism. They don't believe in a Creator, but instead exalt nature itself like it was a god. While I don't agree about there being no creator, I do believe you can get to know God through nature. Through my Montana experiences, I have come to know His awesomeness, His greatness; but most importantly, His love. I mean, whenever I stargaze and I'm lying on my back, staring up at the Milky Way, the enormity of God is revealed, and the beauty and the awesomeness of the display expresses the greatness of His love.

"From Buddhism, I've learned that, through the power of prayer and meditation, God can touch and bring healing to your inner being. Buddhists may not recognize that it's God, but it is.

"From the Jews, I've learned about God's value for community. Go to any big city, and you'll discover that the Jewish community is very tight-knit. They take care of each other."

"Centuries of persecution can have that effect," Chris agrees.

"Absolutely," Diane confirms. "The persecution builds within them the sense of 'it's us against the world, and we must depend upon each other.' But even before all that, it was written in the Torah that God wanted them to be a unified community under His authority. He created laws for only them to follow and holidays they were required to celebrate together.

"I actually find it quite amusing that God felt it necessary to create a mandatory weekly day of rest and required them to have these elaborate festivals of celebration. It's like the Jews were all workaholics who didn't know how to have fun; quite the contrast of today's society."

"I know," he agrees. "Today it's all about getting by with as little work as possible. That's what modern technology has done by making life so much more comfortable and efficient for us."

"Yep. Why even hang around people when you have phones, TVs, and computers to occupy your time? In any case, from Judaism I've learned that God desires people to live in harmony and bond with one another."

"And, of course, God's morality, the thing that always comes to people's minds when thinking about Him, can be found all over many religions. Judaism and Christianity both have the Ten Commandments; Buddhism has the Ten Precepts, and Islam has ten so-called 'moral commandments' to go along with the Five Pillars of Faith. You line those lists up next to each other and you'll find them all strikingly similar. To me, that's clear evidence of God revealing Himself in all faiths," Diane points out.

"So what exactly are you getting at?" he asks. "That all paths lead to God? That even faiths like pantheism and atheism, which don't recognize the existence of a Creator, or ones like Buddhism and Hinduism, which believe in multiple gods and goddesses, will somehow lead you to an actual relationship with the One and Only?"

"Well, yes and no," she answered. "Atheistic and polytheistic faiths may deny the existence of God, but traces of who He is can be found in them. He can even be found in the coldest, dreariest form of atheism. To make the proclamation, 'I don't believe God exists,' requires acknowledging the possibility that He could exist. And when you consider the lengths some of them go to prove God doesn't exist, it leaves you scratching your head wondering, 'Why bother?' In the end, what does it really accomplish?"

"Yeah, and what about those who have a deep hatred towards the belief in God?" Chris asks in a more peaceful tone. "How can you hate something that you don't even believe is real? It seems that their issue is not that He doesn't exist, but that they don't want Him to exist. Because if He did exist, that would mean they couldn't live their lives however they wanted without consequence, like homosexuals. With the possible exception of atheism, no faith that I'm aware of condones homosexuality, and a fair number condemn it. Now, personally, I understand why it's wrong, but at the same time, I wish it wasn't because nobody can choose their feelings. I don't know if they're born that way, or if something happens in life that makes them that way, but I do know that most of them don't want to be that way, but can't seem to change.

"And the reason I say this is because I know what it feels like to be attracted to the same sex. When I was pre-teen, I found myself attracted to both boys and girls. I think it was because boy and girl bodies at that age look the same with only the clothes and haircuts to tell them apart. During those teenage years, however, girls began to develop all those beautiful curves, while boys got hairier and their voices got deeper... disgusting. My attraction to boys quickly soon faded after that," he says somewhat amusingly.

"Anyway," he continues, "so while I'm not attracted to males now, there was a time that I was, and it wasn't by choice. I'd be willing to wager that's how it begins for all pre-teens. And sadly, for whatever reason, some people's affections for the opposite sex fade. Do you know what I'm talking about?"

"I do," Diane confesses. "I admit that I've met a few women to whom I've felt an attraction. However, I knew deep down that if I acted on those feelings that I would fall into bondage, creating more trouble than it was worth. Therefore, I have no regrets.

"And I agree that there's no understanding as to where homosexual feelings come from, but the same can be said about feelings regarding pedophilia, incest, and bestiality. Does that mean we should just deem those behaviors acceptable?"

"No, no, of course not," Chris replies. "A line has to be drawn somewhere, and God has made it clear that anything other than heterosexual, marital sex is wrong. And since He's the Creator of sex, He gets to make the call. Even so, I can't help but feel sorry for those who want to be free from homosexuality, but are just not able.

"But actually, I do understand where those feelings you mentioned ultimately come from. They come from our sin natures. Everybody is born with one and they cause us all to want to go against God's ways. And I'm not talking about just sexual feelings; I'm also talking about feelings of hatred, jealousy, a love for violence, gluttony, drunkenness, greed, cowardice--the list goes on and on. Sin is the most natural thing we do, when put in that perspective, it really shouldn't be surprising about what perversions we humans are capable of indulging."

"That's quite a paradox," she points out. "It shouldn't surprise us because humans have been indulging in perversions since the beginning. God would not have needed to tell the Jews not to do that kind of stuff in the Mosaic Law if it were not taking place. And yet, when we hear about people engaging in it, we are first overcome with shock before disgust settles in."

"You mentioned the Torah earlier. Have you actually read it?" he asks.

"Yes, well, the English version, anyway," she answers.

"The Torah is also part of the Bible. Have you read that?"

"Once in a while, sure. I told you I read a lot of books."

"Have you read a lot of religious books?"

"If you're talking about the religious texts, not really. I've largely read books about religions. The actual texts require a lot of time to study, of which I only have so much."

"Well, what religious texts have you, at least, examined?" he asks.

"Let's see," she says sitting back and looking thoughtfully. "In addition to the Torah and the Bible, there's the Koran, the Hindu Vedas, the Pure Land Sutras, and the Satanic Bible."

Chris's jaw drops when he hears that last item, and he takes a few seconds compose himself so he doesn't wake up the whole house. "Uh, you actually read the Satanic Bible?"

"Yeah. Only 272 pages. I read the whole thing in one weekend."

Still in disbelief Chris says, "And you were trying to find God in that book?"

"Certainly, and I did. I found God's antithesis; the negative to His positive, the yang to His yin, shall we say?" She smiles and then quietly snickers. "No no, I'm kidding. That's not the sort of knowledge I'm ready to have yet."

Chris sighs and says, "That's a relief. Even so, do you believe in the devil?"

"I really can't say, but it wouldn't surprise me considering all the evil that's in this world. How about you?" she asks.

"Absolutely," he replies, "but I'm curious: how can you be uncertain there's a devil if you're so certain there's a God? Both the devil and evil spirits are part of many religions."

"True, but that doesn't prove his existence. There are people involved in such religions that don't really believe in the devil. They simply believe the devil is figurative for man's own evil, and that may be. I just don't know. So what makes you so certain he does exist?" she asks.

"I believe it because the Bible says so," he replies.

"So you're a Christian?"

"I am."

"Somehow I knew you were. How long have you been one?"

"About four years."

"Did you consider all the other faiths out there before choosing Christianity?"

"I didn't have to. God revealed Himself to me completely in the Bible. You mentioned that you've, at least, examined the Bible. Haven't you discovered God in any of it?" he inquires.

"Of course, I have," she replies. "In the Psalms, I read the psalmist's pouring out of love for God in such beautiful, poetic fashion; as well as cries of misery and anguish, and the pleading to God to save him, and the rejoicing of when he is finally rescued. That shows me the love of God, and the intimacy He wants to have with us.

"There's also the Song of Songs. That may be the most beautiful romantic poem I've ever read; definitely inspired by God.

"And then there's Proverbs. Whoa. I would call this the original text of *choose freedom*. It outlines numerous personal choices we make in life and tells us which ones lead to freedom and which ones to bondage. That book is like God's personal confirmation of how I live my life, and that is such a blessing to me.

"Anyway, I'm not saying God doesn't reveal himself in the Bible. He does, just like He does in so many other places. I'm just saying it isn't wise to dismiss every text, or faith just because the first one you examine connects with you. That's pretty closed-minded thinking, and it leads to bondage."

"Really?" Chris reacts. "Even if the Bible really is the inspired Word of God as it says?"

"That's what Muslims say about the Koran," she says in return. "Perhaps if you encountered Islam before Christianity, that's what you'd be proclaiming."

"Alright," he says, "let's just set aside differences in religions for now. You said you don't belong to any particular religion or faith, and that God can be found in any of them, right?"

"That's what I said."

"So let me ask you this: Do you believe there is a heaven?"

"Now that's a good question, one that I've pondered for some time," she responds. "I've considered a number of possibilities regarding the afterlife; including reincarnation and annihilation. Could it be that we've actually lived many past lives and will continue to live them depending on the karma we create in each one? Or is it possible that our souls are not immortal, and we cease to exist after we die, thus making this life our heaven?

"Well, if annihilation is true, that we either instantly become nothing or burn up into nothing when we die, then nothing we do in life matters, which we both agreed upon. Reincarnation on the other hand, implies that there is justice in the world, that there's a reward or punishment for what we do in the present life that carries over into the next one, which means that what we do does matter. But if that's true, then our existence is simply an endless circle of reliving here on earth, and this life that I'm living right now is just one of a potentially infinite number. So just like with annihilation, there's really no ultimate destination, and I just don't see the point of it.

"Besides, to look at reincarnation logically, one would think there would have to be some kind of equilibrium between births and deaths in this world, and yet, births outnumber deaths every day. Furthermore, what if we blow ourselves up with nuclear bombs, or are all wiped out by a giant asteroid? What happens then?

"Therefore, this eternal paradise spoken of in Christianity, Judaism, and Islam seems to be the most likely scenario. So to answer your question: yes, I do believe there is a heaven."

"Alright, do you believe that all people will go to heaven?" Chris asks.

"Wouldn't it be nice if that were true?" she laughs. "But if that were the case, then that would mean Hitler, Stalin and Madeline Murray O'Hare would be hanging out with Moses, the apostle Paul, and Saint Valentine. If God were the good god that I believe He is, I don't believe He would allow that. So I guess not everyone will make it."

"So you also believe there's a hell?" he asks.

"I don't know," she replies. "If we apply yin-yang, then I suppose there would have to be a hell if there's a heaven. But if there is, I can't fathom it being a place of perpetual torment. I would think God would be merciful enough to let them suffer annihilation, a burning up into nothing."

"Hold on. Didn't you just say you didn't accept annihilation?"

"I meant I didn't accept that it was everyone's destiny. The ones who are heaven-bound live forever."

"Well, I certainly hope you're right and annihilation is true, as opposed to eternal torment, but I intend to be in heaven. So what about you? Do you believe you're going to heaven?"

"Of course I do."

"And why do you believe that?"

"Well for starters, I'm no atheist," Diane explains. "I totally believe God exists and I strive to live the good, moral life He wants me to live which He outlines in all major religions."

"Well, it's great that you believe in God," Chris replies. "However, the devil also believes in God and he won't be in heaven. And as for living the good, moral life He desires, how do you know if you've really been good enough?"

"I guess that's what you just call faith, isn't it?" she exclaims in a slightly mocking tone. "Look, God knows my heart. He knows how much I love Him and how thankful I am because I tell Him all the time in prayer. That's what your Bible says to do, right? Pray? Besides, I told you I am already familiar with all the commandments and precepts and I follow them as best I can. My entire philosophy is built on purity; it's what I desire and it's what God wants me to desire. Don't you know that?"

"Of course I do," Chris answers. "That's not the issue. The issue is whether you really are pure. God is perfect, and I believe only those who are without sin can enter His heaven. If you've broken any of those commandments: meaning, if you've ever told a lie, stolen something, loved someone or something more than Him, been lustful or envious toward someone, or ever taken His name in vain, then you are with sin."

"Fine, I'm guilty of doing all those things," she confesses. "Everybody has, including you. But God is forgiving, and I've asked Him to forgive me many times, just as I'm sure you have."

"Yes, God is forgiving," he admits, "and I have asked God to forgive me many times. But God is also a just god. A price has to be paid for any breaking of God's law. Imagine an earthly judge not sending a confessed murderer or rapist to prison simply because he or she asked to be forgiven. That judge would be corrupt, and so would God if that's how He worked."

"Alright," she says, "that's a good point, but if that were really true, then nobody would make it to heaven. But here's the thing, not everybody sincerely seeks God's forgiveness and turns from their evil ways and they will have to pay. I, on the other hand, have done these things."

"I don't doubt you have," he says, "but how do you know you have been forgiven? How can you be so certain that you have escaped God's punishment for your sins?"

Diane's eyes narrow. "Look, I don't know what you want me to say, so why don't you tell me what gives you certainty."

"My certainty lies with my relationship with Jesus Christ," he explains. "In your readings of the Bible, did you ever venture into the New Testament and come across Him?"

"Yes, I do recall reading about Him. He called Himself the Messiah," she says.

"That's right," Chris says. "He did. He was God in the flesh. Unfortunately, nobody believed Him, and He was nailed to a cross and hung there for three hours until He died. Then three days after He died, He was resurrected from the dead and later ascended into heaven. Sound familiar?"

"Yes, that's how the story goes."

"Well, His death on that cross was the payment for my sins. He took my punishment for me. If He hadn't, then I would have had to take it by spending eternity in hell. That is God's gift of redemption. I have received it, and that's why I'm certain I am forgiven."

"As I recall, Christ died for the sins of the whole world, not just yours."

"Yep, that's what John 3:16 says."

"So why isn't everybody going to heaven?" she asks.

"Because not everybody is going to receive the gift," he answers. "You see, a great many don't believe that redemption is through Christ's sacrifice on the cross. And because they don't believe, they don't receive."

"Well, there is one issue I have here," says Diane.

"And that is?" inquires Chris.

"How can you be so certain Christ is the way to redemption?" she asks. "Both Judaism and Islam acknowledge Him as a great teacher or prophet of God, but not the Messiah, so how do you know what's true?"

"I can answer your question based on just one thing: my transformed heart," Chris proclaims. "You see, I know what a heart not transformed by Christ and one that is looks like. I never lost my virginity, but only because I didn't want to get anyone pregnant. Even so, I still pursued girls solely for physical pleasure. I also had no problem being entertained by TV and movies full of sex as well as violence.

"Something else, too; I was my own god. Yeah, I got good grades and played varsity baseball, but it was all to make people look upon me in reverence. I also thought it was hilarious to mock and ridicule weak people to their face and tear others to shreds behind their backs. I loved the feeling of power I felt when I tore down others. I honestly can't believe how selfish I was before Christ saved me."

"And how did that happen?" asks Diane.

"Four years ago, a friend of mine named Kyle and I took a trip to Pittsburgh to see a Penguins game. We arrived several hours before the game to do a little sight-seeing and were walking down Forbes Ave. when suddenly two other guys stepped out from a store entrance in front of us and said, 'Excuse us, guys, but are you saved and if you died tonight are you going to heaven?'

"At first we were both confused. We had no idea what they meant. 'What do you mean are we saved? What are you talking about?' I asked.

"They then shared with us the gospel about how we all are guilty of breaking God's laws and must be punished for it by being sent to hell. But 2000 years ago God came to earth in the form of Jesus Christ and took the punishment meant for every human being, including Kyle and I, so that we can receive forgiveness for our crimes and stand before God blameless at the end of our lives. And the only way to receive it is to believe that Jesus really is who He says He is and did indeed die and rise again and make Him the savior of our lives.

"Well, we both listened politely and took the gospel pamphlets they gave us, but simply walked on, talking about what a weird experience that was. By the time we arrived at the rink for the game we were done talking about any of it. And yet, after arriving back home, I couldn't help but think about that conversation.

"The pamphlets they gave us had the Ten Commandments in them and they really caused me to start examining what kind of person I was. And the more I thought about it, the more it became clear to me that I was guilty of breaking every one, and I swear I was starting to feel afraid, but I couldn't quite convince myself that I was truly lost.

"Then about two months after our trip to Pittsburgh, Kyle called me up. He told me he couldn't stop thinking about that encounter, and that the fear of God had been chewing at him. Desperate for answers, he went to the weekly meeting of First Church Fellowship, a gathering of Christian students on his campus, two nights earlier and he got saved there that evening, and I could tell that something big had indeed happened to him.

"He then started preaching to me about how I needed to be saved, but I told him I wanted to see this group first, so he invited me to come to their next meeting. Well, it didn't take me long to realize there was something different about this bunch. You see, I had always viewed Christians as being these cold and harsh people who never had any fun. But here everyone was filled with this incredible joy and enthusiasm for Jesus. They were genuinely in love with Him, and it was just pouring out of them. I knew I had to have what they had.

"So at the end of the meeting, I asked the leaders, Brian and Angela, to tell me more about Christ, and they shared with me their testimonies about becoming saved and receiving the Holy Spirit, and I swear the Spirit was doing such a work on me. I was now fully convinced of my lost state and knew I needed to get saved.

"However, they made it clear there would be a price to pay to be a Christian, that I had to make Jesus both my Lord as well as my Savior. I couldn't continue being the person I was; I had to allow Jesus to change me into who He wanted me to become and to do whatever it was He wanted me to do. I told them, if that's what I needed to do, then I was ready to do it, and I prayed right there to receive salvation.

"Well, when I did that, this huge feeling of relief just swept through me. I knew something had indeed happened and I told them that. Brian went on to explain that I was indeed saved, but I now needed to start repenting of the sins of my past life; which means confessing to Jesus all of the wrong things I had done, and declare that I didn't want to do them ever again. And he told me to be specific. He said this was necessary to unburden myself from the past and start anew with a clean slate. I wasn't quite comfortable doing that in front of them, but they said it was okay, that I could do it privately if I wanted, and I said I would do it when I got back home.

"So I get back home, and thankfully Kyle came with me, because he had done this himself last week. He told me I should start by going through each of the Ten Commandments, one by one, confess to Christ I was guilty of breaking them many times, identify each incident as they came to mind, and ask forgiveness for each one. I said this would take a while, but he assured me it was necessary.

"So I started with, "You shall not lie", and began to confess whatever lies I had told that came to mind. And as I confessed, God kept bringing more and more lies I had told throughout my life and was feeling His grief over all of them; and when I finally got to the end I was just sobbing over my wicked state…and that was just one of the sins.

"From there, I confessed sins of stealing, lust, hatred, idolatry, pride, selfishness. And on and on it went until about five in the morning when I at last got off my face. I was drained of all my energy, but I was completely renewed. I had a joy inside of me that I had never felt before and I knew then that I was truly saved. Kyle had stayed with me the entire night, and we were just rejoicing together at the end…just incredible."

Chris was giddy with excitement throughout his entire sharing of his testimony, while Diane just sat there stoically, expression unchanged. She remains that way.

"Indeed," she says. "So how have you changed since then?

"For starters," he says, "I'm not a bully anymore. God has made me into a kind person who wants to encourage others. I also don't pursue women with wrong motives either. I now look upon them with honor, the way God intended. He's even laid it on my heart to go apologize to the people I've hurt over the years, and they are always so surprised and thankful to hear it. It's really an incredible witness to what God can do in a person."

"I see. It sounds like you're saying your changed heart and attitude is the evidence of God's forgiveness," she concludes.

"You got it."

"Well then, I must be forgiven, too, because I used to be just like you. I'm guessing you bullied people because you had insecurities, right?"

"I suppose so."

"Well," says Diane, "back in my twenties I got into bodybuilding because I had those same insecurities. I wanted to be noticed, to feel superior to others, so I set out to create a body so unique and so gorgeous that it would make everyone stare in amazement. And when I obtained it, I was more than happy to show it off and put others to shame. You verbally tore people down; I did it nonverbally.

"You also said you pursued women with impure motives while remaining a virgin; I did the same thing with men. During my clubbing days, I used my body to draw many guys to me. I wore clothes that exposed parts of it like my arms and shoulders, and they were so fascinated-- wanting to touch me and me wanting them to.

"I literally kissed about a hundred different guys of every different color. I liked to sample all flavors if you know what I mean," she chuckles. "But in any case, pursuing them only for their affections was both improper and immature. God wanted me to be better than that, and today I am. Therefore, I'm forgiven."

"Oh, I don't doubt that you changed for the better," Chris admits. "The thing is you didn't go through Christ, and therefore have not yet received His forgiveness."

She untucks her legs from underneath and sits straight up. "So you're saying Jesus is the only way to receive God's forgiveness?"

"That's what I'm saying," he says.

"Well I don't see how you can say that and, at the same time, say the evidence of His forgiveness is a changed heart. Islam boasts countless testimonies from young men who lived wicked, wayward lives before becoming Muslims, and are now moral, responsible people. I've also met

Buddhists who used to live lives of worry, strife, and emptiness who found peace and contentment through Buddhism.

"On the other hand, there are plenty of Christians whose lives are full of anger, depression and immorality, and you know that's true. So explain to me how those people have God's forgiveness, and I, along with those aforementioned Buddhists and Muslims don't," demands Diane.

"Because Jesus said, 'I am the Way, the Truth and the Life," Chris replies. "No man can come to the Father except through Me.' By saying that, He eliminated all other routes. I mean, if there were other ways there would've been no need for Him to die such a horrific death on that cross."

Unmoved, Diane tells him, "That's a beautiful piece of theology, but it doesn't answer my question. I'm asking why I should accept your statement that only Christians have God's forgiveness when there are many in other religions that boast changed hearts with the evidence of their transformed lives to back it up while there are plenty of Christians living in complete bondage."

"Right, I'm sorry," he apologizes. "It is true that Islam has changed the lives of many desperate young men by providing them earthly needs like strong, male role-models, a strict moral code, self-respect, and perhaps most importantly, something to live for.

"As for Buddhism, I don't know how it changes people on the inside. Perhaps there is something to all the chanting and prayers, but their powers don't come from God because Jesus is not involved.

"And yes, there are phonies in Christianity today who base their salvation on how good they think they are, or by their church membership and have not been changed on the inside. I admit that it's a shame so many church-going people don't have the dedication and zealousness for Jesus as do those in these false religions who have it for their own gods, philosophies and rituals. You are correct on all those points.

"Nevertheless, living a good, moral life does not make you right with God. Anyone who wants to can choose to make moral choices, and any religion can provide a list of dos and don'ts for living ethically, but it won't bring them forgiveness. There are atheists that live very ethical lives, wouldn't you say?"

"Yes, I agree," she says.

"So what makes you believe you're any different than them?" he asks.

Now Diane is flabbergasted. "Excuse me? Haven't you been listening? I told you that I believe in God."

"This isn't about whether you believe He exits. This is about whether you know Him, have a relationship with Him. Tell me who He is."

"I believe I already told you."

"You told me the reasons you believe He exists. I'm talking about knowing Him on a personal level, beyond simply reading the commandments and precepts found in texts."

"Are you talking about feeling His love for me? I've already told you that, too, about experiencing His love through the five senses. *Taste* and *see* that the Lord is good!" she proclaims pointing her finger upward triumphantly.

"Oh, come on," he responds. "Atheists have those same experiences, too. They just have a different explanation for them. And that 'Montana experience' you're so fond of? I'm sure an atheist could have the same emotional experience you did."

"God loves everybody and speaks to everybody."

"And I believe that, but what I'm saying is someone who is truly right with God, who is truly His child experiences supernatural things that no unbeliever would ever experience."

"Supernatural things…alright, like what?"

"Like an instantly renewed mind and changed heart when one turns from their sins and receives Jesus Christ as his Lord and Savior."

"Oh, this again?" she complains.

"Yes, this again," he responds somewhat harshly. "And I haven't forgotten about your own personal transformation. But there's a huge difference between you and me. You know what that is?"

"Oh, please tell me," she says with obvious sarcasm.

"I've been changed by God and you haven't," he says.

"Really," she again says sarcastically.

"Yes, really," he again replies seriously. "And I know you haven't because you have said as much. When it comes to who you are today, you have given no credit or glory to God. You've given it all to your own created philosophy.

"You may believe in God, but He is not your god. *Choose freedom* is your god. *Choose freedom* is what you turn to as a help…as a guide…

as a savior. I, however, did not turn to any philosophy to learn how to live righteously. I cried out to Jesus in desperation to rescue me from my wickedness and He did it. I no longer desire to do the evil things I once did, and all the glory goes to Him."

Diane is tempted to just get up and walk out right now, but that would look like she was backing down. She can't give up just yet.

"Look," she says as politely as possible, "if Jesus really did miraculously change you, then that's great for you. Perhaps that's the only way you could change. I've done just fine through *choose freedom*. I mean, isn't it possible God used it to make me into the person I'm meant to be?"

"I can't say whether God used it or not," he responds. "There certainly isn't anything wrong with it. However, it's not going to save you from the judgment of your sins. Only Jesus can."

"So you're saying you're going to Heaven, and I'm going to hell even though I've most likely lived a better life than you. That's what you're telling me?"

"Yep, that's it."

"And anyone involved in any other faith other than Christianity is going to hell regardless of how much they've changed for the better. Is that correct?"

"That is correct."

"Well that's just stupid. I mean, how could living a good, moral life not matter to God?"

"I didn't say it doesn't matter. Of course, it matters. What I'm saying is all our good and righteous living does not change the fact that we've also broken God's law many times, and there must be punishment for it. However, Jesus has already taken our punishment, which now allows God to forgive every sin we've ever committed, and what we need to do is receive it."

"And like I've already said, I've sought forgiveness," Diane throws back.

"And like I've already said, you can't be forgiven without receiving what Christ bought for you on the cross: His righteousness," Chris says in return. "No amount of good works or moral living can purchase it. It's a gift from God that you must receive."

"And how do I receive it? By asking?"

"Yes. If you believe in your heart that you are guilty of breaking God's law, and that Jesus died on a cross and was resurrected for your sake, all you have to do is ask and receive."

"I have asked for it. How many more times must I say it?"

"But you have not yet believed in your heart that Jesus died and was resurrected for your sake. And you have not surrendered control of your life to Him. You must do that to be saved."

"What do you mean, 'surrender control of my life'?"

"I mean just that. You choose to give up the right to control your own life and become a humble servant of Jesus Christ. He bought your salvation with His blood and His life, and if you want to receive it, He has to own you."

She stares at him with a look of disbelief. "Own me?" she says quietly but with obvious contempt. "As in give up my freedom to choose and become a puppet on a string? Oh now you're talking crazy here. No way in the world, God, my creator, would want me to be a puppet. No way."

"Why not?" he asks very calmly.

Diane's frustration with him has now reached its boiling point as she bites her tongue. She knows this is about to get ugly, so she quickly stands up, motions to him to come with her, and walks to the sliding door. Chris responds by getting up and following her out. He slides the door closed behind them.

"Why not?!" she exclaims in a hard voice. "Because He gave me a free will! Why would He do that if He wants to control me?"

"First of all, nobody is a puppet to God," he calmly explains. "We always have a choice. He never forces anybody to obey Him. The ones who are saved, who are surrendered to Him, will freely choose to obey His commandments out of love for sending His Son to die for us."

"So now we're back to the commandments again? It's amazing how we keep coming back to where we started."

"Yes, I suppose so. But now I believe we've reached the ultimate question: What is the motivation of your heart?"

"What do you mean?"

"Do you strive to follow God's commandments out of love or pride?"

"Are you questioning whether I love God? I already told you I do."

"I'm sure you do, to a degree. But is it possible that you love other things more, like your philosophy? Are you familiar with the Pharisees in the Bible?"

"I've heard of them."

"They were teachers of God's law in Israel," he says to her. "They believed in God and followed the commandments better than anybody. Everyone looked upon them as the standard-bearers for godly living. And yet, while Jesus gently dealt with known thieves and prostitutes, He was very harsh when dealing with the Pharisees. And why was that? It was because they didn't believe there was anything wrong with them; that they were o.k. the way they were and didn't need anybody's help. Therefore, Jesus had to be harsh with them to make them realize their own sins of greed, lust, and lack of love in their hearts. The thieves and the prostitutes, on the other hand, already knew they were evil and in need of a savior. And so my point is, you can be the best commandment keeper in the world and still have an evil heart."

"So what are you getting at?" she demands.

"What I'm getting at is you strike me as a modern-day Pharisee," he now says sternly. "You think you're fine the way you are; that you've done all the work necessary to make yourself worthy of His forgiveness; that you've made yourself into this incredibly magnificent person that God finds impressive. There is nothing about you, or anything you've done that He finds impressive. When you're the creator of the universe, how could you possibly be impressed by any human accomplishment?"

"Hey, I'm not proclaiming myself as impressive," she says defiantly.

"Yes, you are," he responds. "You've been doing it ever since you sat down with me over there and started talking about the stars. You've been boasting about what a moral, enlightened, and well-traveled person you are, and what a life changing philosophy you've created."

"I was just telling you about myself and how I found meaning in life. If that intimidates you then I'm sorry."

"This isn't about intimidation; it's about making you realize that you aren't on the pathway to heaven. With all your righteous living you are full of something that God despises: pride. Now I realize you said *choose freedom* requires humility, but you're talking about living a humble lifestyle, and that does not make you humble at heart."

"That's not true!" she shouts angrily. "The fact that I'm content with living humbly proves I'm humble at heart!"

"Well, to be honest," he says calmly, "I'm not so sure you really do live humbly. One could look at all these 'Montana experiences' you've taken and call that pretty extravagant." Chris then looks at her square in the face and says, "And let me ask you something else: What's your attitude towards people who aren't as "free" as you are? Do you look down upon them? Do you thank God you're not like them? Do you think you're better than them?"

Diane is stunned silent by the conviction of these questions. She knows the truth, and it's not in her to lie about it.

"I...suppose I do," she says after the mustering up of her will to admit it.

"Well that's exactly the kind of attitude the Pharisees had regarding all the people Jesus hung around with. In fact, they were appalled that He associated with people they considered 'scum.' And yet, He told them that this 'scum' would enter heaven before they would.

"Why did He say that? Because they were at a point in their lives where they knew they couldn't make themselves acceptable before God and, therefore, needed Him to save them. But the Pharisees were far from that point, trusting in their own righteousness to stand accepted before God, rather than realizing they, too, needed a savior.

"Now, as for you, you may think you're acceptable based on your own standards, but how do you think you're going to stand up to God's standard, which is perfection? What makes you think that you don't need a savior while someone like me does?"

That's enough. Diane is done having her character, her integrity, and especially her philosophy be attacked by some punk know-it-all she met on the beach.

"Alright alright, perhaps in my pursuit of freedom I have become a little too proud. Thank you for pointing that out, but as for this conversation, it's done! Over! Finished! You don't want to embrace my beliefs? That's fine! Go ahead and suffer!"

She starts to turn, but then whips back around and says intensely, pointing her finger at him, "Oh, as for Jesus being the only way to heaven, I can't prove that you're wrong, but let me tell you something. For God to only create one way to salvation when He wants to save everybody just doesn't add up, especially when you can find Him in so many other faiths. And another thing, we all will have to give an account of our lives to Him when our time comes, and when I do see Him, I will be able to truthfully say that I did my best to live the way He wanted me to live. And now it's really time for me to get going. Thank you and have a nice life," she says angrily, then turns and starts walking away.

"Wait a minute," Chris calls to her.

Diane turns back around and shouts. "No! We're done here!"

"Diane…wait!!"

She sighs. "What?"

He walks up to her. "I want you to consider something real quick."

"Which is what?" she says flustered.

"Does any of this make sense to you?"

"What are you talking about?" she asks.

"All of this," he replies. "You come back from an evening of stargazing and see a complete stranger sitting on a beach paying you no mind, somebody you have no reason to speak to at all, and all of a sudden you decide to sit down and tell your life story to him for an entire evening. You know that just doesn't add up logically, and yet that's what you did. What in the world made you decide to stop what you were doing and have this conversation?"

Her head drops, and she shrugs her shoulders. "I don't know," she says shaking her head. "I honestly don't know. When I first saw you sitting there, I had no interest in stopping to talk. I was just going to walk right past, and yet something told me I should stop and find out about you. Applying *choose freedom*, I knew that if I didn't stop to talk to you, I would be driving home wondering who you were and wishing I had stopped, which would've meant being in bondage. So, I took the chance."

"Something stopped you. Is it possible that is was God Himself who stopped you?"

"It may have been. It also may have been basic human compassion for a lonely-looking person. I just don't know."

"Well it was God who stopped you…and I can prove it."

Her eyes widen, her mouth slackens a bit, and she again holds her finger up at him.

"You can prove that God arranged this encounter," she slowly exclaims. "You now have my complete attention."

"I'm going to show you my driver's license," says Chris.

He reaches into his pocket. Diane instinctively places her hand on her pocket containing her switchblade.

"What?! What are you doing?"

He takes out his wallet, pulls out his driver's license and hands it to her.

"Look at my birth date."

"Oh, what kind of stupidity is this?"

"Look at it."

"Chris, I don't even want to know your last name, much less when you were born!"

"I'm not asking you to look at anything but my birth date. Trust me; you'll understand when you see it."

She sighs. "Oh, alright; fine," she says taking it. "I'm only looking at your birth date."

Diane walks back on the deck and holds the license up to the light coming through the sliding door. At first she squints, but soon her eyes widen, and a look of absolute shock covers her face. She then looks back at Chris and covers her mouth with her hand.

"You figured it out, didn't you?" says Chris to Diane. "I did, too, the second I read the date on the back of your bracelet. At first I was going to say something, but God spoke to me in my heart telling me to wait. Now I see why.

"Diane, I'm a first-time visitor to this place. I've never sat on this beach before this night, a night that would bring you out here to stargaze, and at just the time you would be returning. This is probably the only time our paths would ever cross. And then you show me a bracelet that just happened to have *that* date engraved on it? You had mentioned possibly being predestined to be here earlier. Well, do you see the absolute perfection of this encounter?"

Diane says nothing. Chris then continues.

"We talked earlier about finding meaning and purpose in life. Well, it seems God's purpose for me was to have this encounter, this conversation with you. And if that be the case, and I die at dawn in the morning, then

I will enter eternity thankful for my life and that I did what I was created to do.

"Diane, the Lord is all knowing and He knew before you were even born the path you would travel and that you would need someone there to show you the true way when the time was right. And the day you started down the path that you thought would lead you to salvation was the day He created that someone for that time…this time.

"Diane, the Lord desperately desires your soul. He desperately desires to have intimacy with you and to forgive you of your sins. But the only way you can receive all that is to believe that Christ died and rose for you and to surrender yourself to His lordship. It really is the only way. That's why He's created this encounter for you, just for you. So do you believe that, Diane? Are you ready to listen?"

Diane continues to stare at him for a few more seconds, then slowly nods her head.

AFTERMATH

THE DATE IS WEDNESDAY, August 22nd, 2012. Diane Marie Carnes sits in the first-class section of a flight to Pensacola, Florida, looking very prim and proper in her white silk blouse, brown pleated skirt, and suede boots. She has never flown first-class before, but decided she should do it at least once in her life. While the cost hurt a little bit, she loves the wide comfortable seats with tons of leg-room in front of her, not to mention the peacefulness of the flight because only four others are flying in her section.

Diane is flying out to see her two best friends, Corinne Sasha Martelli and Dawn Robinson Keller, for their annual get-together. Once every year, for the last seven years, the trio abandons their regular lives for a few days to gather in a city none of them have ever resided in to enjoy each other's company, just like in the old days. This is the only time of the year Cori ever takes time off from her tour schedule, and Dawn is without either her husband or children. None of them would miss this gathering for the world. It's a time for the three of them to rekindle the excitement of their twenties while becoming acquainted with who they are today.

Cori will, no doubt, be sharing stories about her life on tour from the past year and always having just enough money to scrape by. It's astounding, really. Diane had so prided herself on being free from materialism because she chose to live an austere lifestyle, yet she still brought home healthy paychecks and kept most of what she made. Cori, however, has no choice but to live in austerity and she is perfectly content because she is doing what she loves. Cori is the one who is truly free in that area, Diane now realizes.

Dawn won't be flying in, instead opting to take the train since she is now five months pregnant with her fourth baby girl. Four girls! What a jackpot! It's truly mind-boggling how Dawn seems to get everything she desires: her looks, her personality, her husband, and now having all girls. She has simply never been in want.

Dawn called Diane with the wonderful news about four weeks ago, wanting to wait until she and Shane knew their child's gender. She said they were off-the-wall excited that they were having a fourth daughter, and that their girls were thrilled to be getting another sister. While happy for Dawn, Diane could only hang her head for herself as she soaked in her friend's joy.

Diane always knew Dawn was happy in her life, but had also considered herself more enlightened and fulfilled since she was free from the responsibilities of being a wife and mother. And yet, for all the knowledge and wisdom she's gained from her books, articles, films, documentaries and travels, none of those things had ever provided her with love. Knowledge and wisdom have never cared for her, never encouraged her, never comforted or believed in her. It is so true that without love, you gain nothing.

Dawn has it; her brothers have it; and Cori has it, too, because her dance troupe is a second family to her. Diane, however, in her pursuit of a bondage-free life, had ironically built a prison of isolation for herself. Oh, how the wise are made foolish.

And yet whatever great things her friends have to report about their lives, Diane knows they will all pale in comparison with what she has to tell. She is going to reveal to them how God Almighty drew her to the Way of true salvation and eternal life, Jesus Christ. She recorded every detail of that night in her 78th diary, which she is rereading and reliving at the moment.

When she saw Chris's birth date on his license, the fear of God swept through her quickly. She had read about Him and prayed to Him for years, but that night He, without question, got up close and personal and called out to her. There was no choice in the matter; she had to respond.

There on the beach house deck, Chris shared with her the message of God's grace through faith in Jesus Christ; that if she, by faith, handed control of her life over to Him, He would give her His righteousness in return. As she listened, the conviction of God fell upon her and revealed the lost state of her heart. The weight of conviction rapidly built upon her to the point of being unbearable. She needed relief and began to believe that Jesus was ready to give it to her.

But when Chris asked if she now believed what the Bible said about Him was true and if she wanted to surrender control of her life to Him, a battle raged within her. For so many years she had believed the key to freedom was the ability to have complete control over one's life, and anything less than that was bondage. This idea of Jesus being in control of her life, being in submission to Him, went against everything she believed as truth. She couldn't have been wrong all this time, could she?

And yet here she was in an encounter that had been prearranged by God Himself. It was impossible to deny it. Would she be so stubborn as to refuse to consider the possibility that giving up control of her life was really the key to freedom? The irony would be if she didn't consider it she would be going against *choose freedom*. She had to give Jesus a chance.

So with every ounce of faith she had in her heart, she bowed her face to the ground, confessed her sinful state, and called out to Jesus to take her life and save it. When she did that, all the fear immediately left her and she was filled with a sense of peace. She raised her head and revealed a look of genuine surprise and relief on her face. Something supernatural had indeed happened.

"You just got saved, didn't you?" he said as he looked upon her.

She slowly nodded her head and whispered, "Yes, I think so."

Chris then said the next step was to start confessing her sins individually to Jesus and receive His forgiveness. Diane remembered him say he started with lies when he began his process, so she did the same. At first, her confessing came slowly, but then the Spirit began to bring more and more sins to light. Soon the confessions began to pour out of her mouth as she groaned over her realized state of wickedness. It was unbelievable. For two straight hours, the Spirit made her recall things she did as a child all the way to the angry feelings she felt towards Chris right before he handed her his driver's license.

Under His conviction, she realized she had committed fornication in her heart with all those men she kissed in those clubs despite not sleeping with any of them. To her surprise, He also revealed that her morality and clean lifestyle were idols to her. She had trusted in them for her salvation and not in Christ.

Finally, the moment she knew was coming came: the renouncing of *choose freedom*. It broke her heart to hear this. *Choose freedom* was her creation, her brainchild, her baby; the thing her life had revolved around since age fifteen. It was her pathway to understanding life, good and evil, and God Himself. It was what she trusted in to gain peace, prosperity, protection and purpose in life. It was her savior.

The very idea of confessing something she had poured all that she was into as an idol and a path that led to destruction was unbearable. She was on her face in anguish at the realization that she had deceived herself for all those years. Her pride and the Spirit raged a fierce war inside her, and she groaned in agony.

Thank goodness Chris was there to comfort and encourage her, even though she hated looking helpless in front of him. He kept assuring her that she needed do it because she couldn't serve two masters, and of the two, only Jesus will love her back.

Finally, when the conviction overcame her pride, she muttered, with her face buried in her arms, that she renounced *choose freedom* as her god and declared Jesus Christ was her Lord and Savior. When she did that, she suddenly became flooded with feelings of love and joy that were beyond comprehension. It was truly finished.

When she got home that night at around 4 a.m., she immediately rushed to her diary and began frantically writing all that had happened, and that she truly felt reborn. She finished writing near sunrise and, while exhausted, she was still feeling as alive as ever. Thank goodness it was Sunday, and she didn't have to go to work, but she knew she needed to go to church.

She got down on her knees and told God she wanted to get baptized that morning, asking if He would please tell her where to go. Within seconds, a church popped into her mind. She couldn't recall the name, but she had driven past it a few times.

After she showered and dried off, she put on a bathing suit with a white polo shirt and shorts over top, along with white socks and tennis shoes. She then drove to the church and arrived as Sunday school was in session. When she found the pastor, she told him about getting saved the previous night and asked if she could get baptized that day. It turned out the church had a baptism pool, and he would be happy to do it right then if she wanted.

Twenty minutes later, she was in the pool with the pastor, who was wearing waders, and in the name of the Father, the Son, and the Holy Spirit, was baptized in front of all the Sunday school attendees. They were the first ones to hear her testimony, which is what she has been sharing for the last four months.

Two weekends after she got saved, she drove down to her parents' house in North Carolina and told them about what had happened. Both of them attended church while growing up, but neither felt they needed God nor the church in their lives when they became adults. So when they heard their daughter's testimony, it sounded a little too wild to them at first.

However, they definitely sensed something was very different about Diane. The most startling evidence of this change being that their daughter had renounced *choose freedom*, telling them it ultimately led to the glorification of herself as an idol, thus putting her in a bondage of pride. They both knew that her self-created philosophy was what she held most dear in her life for so long, so to hear her now say true freedom was found in Jesus Christ meant something beyond belief had indeed taken place.

Diane hasn't seen her brothers yet; although she has talked to them on the phone and they also realize something has definitely happened to her. She still has yet to tell them (or anyone else, for that matter) about her contemplation of suicide, but now knows that she must. They need to realize how God used them to save her life. There's no question in her mind He did.

She chose to wait to share the news of her conversion with Cori and Dawn for this get-together because she wanted to do it face-to-face. When she arrives they may notice something's different right away. For starters, she has removed her *choose freedom* ID bracelet (it now lays in her jewelry box), which she wore for almost as long as she's known them, and replaced it with one that says "Born Again," with "April 21, 2012" engraved on the back. She has also ditched the yin-yang pendant for a simple gold cross around her neck. But what she hopes they notice is the aura of goodness and mercy that surrounds her now.

She closes the diary and begins to reflect upon who she has become during these last four months. She is still committed to being completely clean of smoking, alcohol, drugs, and premarital sex, now vowing to never even kiss a man who is not her husband. The difference is she now does it out of love for God rather than for selfish pride. She's gone from learning about God to actually knowing Him; from loving Him for what He does to loving Him for who He is; from striving for freedom to actually being free. And it's all because God loved her so much that He gave His only begotten Son so long ago to save her.

Furthermore, in spite of there being more than seven billion people in the world, He cared enough for her to create and send someone into her life to show her the way to Him. In fact, it goes beyond just Chris. Her parents, Daniel and Donovan, Todd, Cori and Dawn; God used them all, and who knows who else, to save her from destruction. It brings her to tears nearly every time she ponders that amazing love.

Yet even though God has made significant changes in her already, there is still much more to accomplish. There are still a few strongholds in her life that need to be torn down, and the biggest one is pride.

It was so hard to believe at first, but the truth is undeniable: *choose freedom* was never really about freedom, but about pride. It was about being better than everybody else; becoming so smart, so sophisticated, so healthy, so generous, so independent, so self-confident, so diligent, so creative…so free…that people would look upon her in amazement. To become someone of such perfection that God Himself would find her worthy of Heaven. Thank the Lord she can see the truth now.

But while she's now humble enough to admit she deserved hell and needed a redeemer, she still has this independent spirit inside of her. She still has feelings of superiority towards others and not wanting to submit to anyone, which is probably why she's never married.

Donovan once told her that she was the last person in the world he expected to ever marry. She remembered wanting to smack him for that, but is in total agreement now. In spite of all she ever said about being open to marrying, she had believed that the key to happiness was making oneself smart and strong while never having to rely on anybody else.

For so long she's loved being unmarried and chaste, and still loves it, but if that is God's desire for everyone, then the whole human race would quickly die out. It's astounding that she could have been that arrogant.

Still, there are a few that God calls to remain unmarried for His sake, and she told Him she was ready to be such a person. However, her prideful, independent spirit needed to die, and killing it would be a long, painful process requiring some extreme measures. So instead of letting her remain where she was most comfortable, God instead chose for her to become the wife of a dairy farm mechanic fifteen years her junior, something she never in a million years would've fathomed happening.

As she glances at the engagement ring Christopher Todd Blackman slipped onto her finger five days ago, she rolls her eyes and the back of her head hits the head rest as she ponders the insanity of her falling in love and wanting to marry someone like him. Yes, she does love him and wants to be married to him, but who hasn't felt that way at the start of any marriage, good or bad? Logically speaking, marrying him would be a huge mistake.

But even though she's literally shaking in her boots at the thought of marrying Chris, she knows in her spirit this is God's destiny for her, for both of them. In fact, in retrospect, she sensed it the day after she got baptized. If He made Chris for her sake, then surely she could've been made for Chris's sake, too. His ways are certainly not her ways, but they're always better.

Her mind doesn't comprehend why her heart desires Chris; however, when God transforms the heart, all things are possible. Yes, all things are truly possible. And as she renews her mind to the ways of God and leans not on her own understanding, she'll soon see it's going to be alright.

She fingers the cross around her neck, closes her eyes, and prays, "I am a new creature in Christ. My old life is passed away, and my new life will be glorious."

EPILOGUE

IT IS NOVEMBER OF 2015. Diane and Chris have now been married three years and presently reside in rural Pennsylvania with their nineteen-month old identical twin daughters, Linda and Heidi.

In the wedding Diane was clothed head to foot entirely in pure white; wearing a calf-length skirt, blouse, waist sash, satin gloves, dress jacket, leather boots, and hairband. She would've refused to have worn white had she not been a virgin, and had rejoiced in her worthiness to wear it, but even more so, in receiving a pure groom by the graciousness of God.

The ceremony had gone off without a hitch, and their honeymoon in Nassau was absolutely impeccable. Diane had indeed lived out every girl's fantasy. But when they returned home from Nassau, the fantasy ended. She knew she was now entering a lengthy period of sacrifice and being broken. So far, her expectations have been met.

For starters, she's found out that Chris is far from perfect. He's a hardworking provider, loving father, and faithful lover but was still a very young adult with a lot of immaturity to overcome; which was her greatest fear about marrying him. This probably wouldn't have been noticeable to her if they were around the same age but that's very much not the case.

She knows he'll mature as he gets older, but so far it's been very difficult for her to respect his position of head of the household. Her role is to be his helper, and she's helped him any and every way she can. However, her desire to take charge and tell him what to do has led to many stressful periods.

Then there was the utter shock of becoming a new mother at age forty to identical twins. Finding out she was pregnant on the brink of middle-age certainly surprised her, but finding out she was having twins left her dumbstruck. She thought twins skipped a generation, but that's fraternal, not identical. So after twenty-two straight years of adulthood with no dependents, she suddenly found herself with two infants at an age where many mothers have kids in high school.

That also meant her having to quit her job as a media center assistant at a nearby elementary school to become a full-time mom. She already gave up her cushy law librarian job to move to rural Pennsylvania. Now she had to leave the workforce altogether and be completely dependent on Chris to provide for everything.

That was completely foreign to her. In fact, it was downright scary. Yes, she was already quite used to living very simply, but now there wasn't any choice.

So far Chris has had to put in a lot of ten and, sometimes, twelve-hour days to make ends meet, and she misses him daily. Thankfully, he won't work on Sundays, but she wished he could be at home helping her with the twins regularly because she's felt so overwhelmed.

After the twins were born, Diane's life primarily consisted of feedings, changings, cleaning up messes, taking the babies places, keeping them entertained--everything under the sun when it comes to raising babies and seemingly doing it all by herself. There was no time for a lot of those pleasures she enjoyed when she was single. She rarely even wrote in her diary because of a lack of time and inspiration. She's said, 'I'm too old for this,' more times than she can count.

And why did they have to be girls? What would she know about raising girls? She grew up with two little brothers and related to boys better, so why didn't God give her boys? Oh sure, Chris has always wanted daughters and is beyond thrilled to finally have them, but he's not the one staying at home with them.

Things finally came to a head one afternoon last October, shortly before their second anniversary. Diane was sitting at the kitchen table trying to enjoy a cup of hot tea after quieting the girls down, but all her frustrations had built to the point where she couldn't contain them anymore. She suddenly burst into tears, buried her face in her arms on the table, and cried out to God in anguish.

"God, this isn't fair!" she sobbed. "I'm the one making all the sacrifices here! I have given up everything for him and I'm miserable! Is this really the life you wanted for me?!"

God let her cry for a few minutes before He quietly spoke to her heart. He acknowledged she had indeed given up everything, but it hadn't been for Chris, it had been for Him. He reminded her that He had ordained their marriage; that this was His will, and to follow it required giving up everything she had.

She remembered something she had read in her Bible and went and got it. She opened it up to the Gospels and found the story of the rich young ruler who was told by Jesus to sell all his possessions and follow

Him. She then turned to the sixteenth chapter of Matthew and reread the section on denying herself, picking up her cross and following Him and losing her life to save it. That sounded just like her life at that point, and her demeanor brightened.

"Alright Lord," she said out loud. "If I understand this correctly, I'm right where you want me to be. What happens next?"

He then told her He had accomplished what she knew from the beginning: break her independent spirit. She confessed that she had now reached a state of complete brokenness and was willing to accept the truth that she could not continue any further with just her own strength. What she had to do now, she figured, was ask Him to help her with every task for the rest of her days, because apart from Him, she could do nothing.

"Oh, Lord God, I thank you that I'm not outside your will. I thank you that my willingness to give up everything is what you desire of me. I will definitely start relying more on you from here on out."

She thought that was the end and started to get up, but then she felt what seemed like an invisible hand on her shoulder. She took it to mean God wasn't done, and He wasn't. When she sat back down, He addressed the other issue she brought up: that she was the only one making sacrifices. He laid out for her that it was definitely not the case.

For starters, it hadn't been easy for Chris to live with a wife that had not yet been broken and submissive. He brought to her mind several instances where she challenged his authority on a number of family decisions mainly because she didn't have confidence in him. He asked her if she had ever considered what it must be like for Chris to have his wife treat him like he couldn't handle being the head of the household.

God also reminded her that Chris had gone from providing for only himself to taking care of a family of four while working the same job for the same wages. Did she actually believe all those extra hours he put in were no big deal to him? That he really would rather be at work than at home with her and their precious twins?

Diane's heart sank with these revelations. She had thought she was the only one enduring suffering in this marriage. She now realized that she had been so wrapped up in herself and her own issues and struggles that she hadn't been paying any mind to her husband's feelings, and how her attitudes and actions had been affecting him.

God showed her that she looked down on Chris because she saw herself as the smarter, more mature person, and that she was subtly spilling that attitude onto Chris in the form of correction and criticism while offering very little encouragement.

And yes, she had selfishly believed that she was the only one with money concerns. Surely Chris was baring a burden himself, and she had not been making things easier for him. Her self-pity started to fade at that point. She needed to repent.

"Dear Lord, I confess that I have been treating Chris unfairly. I have been blaming him for things that are beyond his control and not respecting his position as head of this family. Please forgive me. I will apologize to him for this."

Again she started to get up, but again felt that hand on her shoulder. God still wasn't done. He then ran down that lengthy list of gripes that she had made up in her mind were contributing to her misery. He then pulled no punches.

You hold bitterness towards Linda and Heidi. You blame them for your misery. You resent them for having to give up so much for the sake of caring for them. You see motherhood as a burden and not a joy and believe it's their fault. You even resent them for not being boys.

That accusation stung Diane. She shot up from her chair and pointed her finger upward.

"How dare You! How dare You say that to me! How dare You not have sympathy for me after all I've done for them! I never even asked for twins! You're the one who decided to put them in my life and have me care for them! IT'S YOUR…" She paused in mid-sentence as it quickly hit her as to what her next word was going to be.

For several seconds, Diane stood there frozen in shock at what just came out of her mouth, and then she quietly sat down and automatically turned in her Bible to Genesis, chapter 3. God had asked Adam if he had eaten the forbidden fruit, and Adam's reply was, 'The woman You gave to be with me, she gave me of the tree, and I ate.' (NKJV) Suddenly guilt rushed into Diane like a flash flood as she put her hands on the sides of her head and wadded up fistfuls of her hair.

"No, no, no," Diane whispered to herself at the realization that she actually did hold bitterness toward her innocent, then six-month old twins, and even toward God Himself. The burden was so much that she couldn't even sit. She slid off the chair onto the floor and onto her knees. She folded her hands, closed her eyes, and began to pray in pure desperation.

"Dear Lord, I am so sorry. I am sorry for how I've treated my girls. None of this is their fault; they've done me no wrong. Please forgive my resentment. And I realize, Lord, that ultimately I've blamed You for my misery and I'm sorry. Oh, please forgive me for my selfishness. Please, change my heart, Lord. Please help me to love Chris and the girls the way they deserve. And, Lord, please help me to love You like I'm supposed to. Please help me."

She just kept on praying and praying right there on the floor for God to forgive her and change her heart. Then, after it felt like a half-an-hour had passed, she felt the burden suddenly lift off. Diane then lifted her head upwards, raised her hands in praise, and worshipped her Lord who makes all things new.

When she got up, she quickly rushed into the girls' room and looked down in Linda's crib at her daughter's sunny face. Diane flashed a big smile right back at Linda and reached down and picked her up. Holding the baby against her chest, Diane stroked the back of the child's head and quietly said, "I'm sorry, baby. Mommy's sorry. I really do love you." A few minutes later she did the same with Heidi.

That evening, Chris arrived home from work just after seven to find his wife standing in the kitchen with a supper of baked lamb chops seasoned with curry powder and a fresh orzo salad waiting for him. "There's Rocky Road ice cream for dessert," she told him. He was quite pleased. Diane wasted no time.

"Chris, I'll get right to it. I have not respected you as head of this household. I have been criticizing and correcting you rather than encouraging you. Sweetheart, you've been doing the best you can, which is all I can ask of you, and I thank you for that. Will you forgive me?"

Chris' head dropped, and he put his hand to his forehead. He then looked up at her with a humbled expression and held his arms out to her. Diane walked over and joined him in a loving embrace. There was silence for a bit before Chris broke it.

"You have no idea how badly I needed to hear that. Thank you," he said to her.

"I know. I know," she whispered, stroking the back of his head.

Later, after eating, he admitted that he had not been sensitive to all she had given up for their family and asked her forgiveness. She happily forgave him as another burden was lifted.

Since that day, she has been on her face daily, praying to God, begging Him to fill her with His strength and His Spirit. She faithfully searches the Word for wisdom and understanding, seeking it with her whole heart as Proverbs 2:1-6 ordains. She also regularly recites the 23rd Psalm to assure herself that the Lord is leading her family through these tough times. In return, He has given her the strength, wisdom and anointing she needs to make it through each day.

In addition, she and Chris take time to pray together daily, laying on hands and praying blessings over each other, and on their daughters. Furthermore, since that day of correction, Diane has seen God use her loved ones to help her through her myriad of trials.

First there's Cori, who knows all about getting by on very little and still loving life. Diane has unburdened herself a number of times to her about money worries, and Cori has responded with empathy and encouragement for which Diane is very thankful.

Then there's Dawn, who has been happily sharing with Diane her wisdom on raising and understanding girls, as well as stories of the joy they bring to one's life. Dawn regularly tells Diane of the fulfillment her twins will bring, which is exactly what Diane needs to know.

And, of course, there's Diane's own family. Her parents know all about raising twins, and her brothers know plenty about being twins. They have all been graciously sharing their wisdom and insight with her. Furthermore, Donovan and his wife recently welcomed their first child, a son, into the world; so all three siblings are now sharing parenting stories.

In the last dozen years she has never been closer with all her loved ones than she is today, and God has made it happen through her struggles. It's become so clear why God made her a full-time mom of twin girls: to bless her. This was His perfect will coming to fruition.

She now *whole-heartedly* gives God thanks for Linda and Heidi. She couldn't do that during the first few months of their lives, but the truth has set her free.

She's even inspired to journal again. Her personal times with God have resulted in her writing many letters, both of love and anguish, to Him. She is presently on diary #83 and expects to reach #100 before age fifty. It'll probably be time to start writing that book by then, though she's now uncertain as to what it will be about.

All glory goes to God, for this is His perfect will. In fact, He predestined this life for her for one ultimate purpose: to create a testimony that brings glory to Him.

She and Chris share their testimony both individually and as a couple with others fairly regularly. Whenever an opportunity pops up, they seize it. Their boldness comes from the Holy Spirit within them and the power of their testimony.

Some people don't want to hear it, but those that do are always astounded by how God saved them both and brought them together. They testify that their marriage was ordained by God, and it couldn't possibly survive without God being in control. When the others they talk to take in what an unlikely pairing they are, few can disagree.

Chris and Diane have talked about possibly buying an RV and taking a road trip through the States, stopping in towns throughout the country to share their testimony. They're not quite at peace with that idea yet, but they may be doing some other traveling soon.

One evening in the kitchen last week, while Diane was putting away the clean dishes, Chris walked in and asked her what she thought about possibly moving back to North Carolina to be closer to her family and friends. For the second time in their marriage, she was left dumbstruck.

She then quickly rushed to him and jumped into his arms, causing him to stumble backwards hard into the kitchen counter. He took that as an answer in the affirmative. Chris still needs to find work down there, but the two are confident that God will provide him something when it's His time.

In her old life, the world was at Diane's fingertips. She was constantly gaining knowledge, had no 'needless' responsibilities, and was free to travel the earth on a whim.

Today, her life is like that of many stay-at-home moms. She's read maybe seven books in the last three years, and all the money she had saved for future 'Montana experiences' is now her family's rainy day fund. All that she once held dear is now lost, yet she misses none of it.

Before her salvation, she was constantly running after something: the next book, the next experience, the next breakthrough, the next victory. There was always something out there she was craving. Today there's no more chasing, for she now resides in a house full of God's love.

Diane has finally found her destiny: to be a child of God and to reside in His will. The world is no longer hers; she is now His…for all eternity. Amen.

THE END